TEMPERED IRON

Steve Sherman

Walker and Company
New York

First published in the United States of America in 1989
by Walker Publishing Company, Inc.

Published simultaneously in Canada by Thomas Allen & Son
Canada, Limited, Markham, Ontario

Library of Congress Cataloging-in-Publication Data

Sherman, Steve, 1938-
Tempered iron / Steve Sherman.
ISBN 0-8027-4100-2
I. Title.
PS3569.H4337T46   1989
813'.54—dc20   89-35270
CIP

Printed in the United States of America

2   4   6   8   10   9   7   5   3   1

CHAPTER 1

HE watched the rider weave his bay mare in and out the scrub brush and head for his cabin. He watched him come easy up the long, simmering slope, and the closer the rider came, the clearer he could see the newness in him. The man rode with a kind of dusty, shiny surface—on the loose but too stiff in the saddle. His pants creases were gone, his yellow shirt hung close to his skin, but the lines of his body hadn't yet fitted to the country.

Still watching through the window, he reached by habit for his holster on the table. He wrapped the fitted leather around his waist and, eyes kept up, bent to tie the cord around his lower thigh, tightening the bottom of the holster so that it would move with his leg, not on its own.

Then he stepped to the open door where the dry sagey breeze filtered through the inside of the low cabin and out the back window. He stayed in the darkness of the doorway; he would appear to be a shadowy form to the rider out in the bright sun.

No one came to this place by accident. The rider must have gone into town and asked for him.

Caliente was small enough. People knew who lived in close and who lived in the outlying country alone. Nine out of ten drifters went into the Road's End Saloon, and this kid was probably one of them. If somebody didn't tell him where the cabin was for a cheap whiskey, the bartender Hank did. Or Doc.

The kid reined up twenty feet in front of the cabin. He was too trusting, hadn't learned to be cautious or he would

1

have reined in double or triple that, and away from an open door so as not to show himself.

"Jack?" the kid called out tentatively.

He let the rider wait, shift some in the saddle, and look around toward the side of the cabin.

"Jack? You there?"

The dust settled at the mare's hooves by the time Jack stepped from the door frame into the sun. Up close the kid was thinner than the vibrating heat made him out to be in the distance. He was skinny, probably hadn't eaten much lately. His boots were scuffed, but not really worn. His beige broad-brimmed hat and shirt were bright for reflecting the hot sun on a cowhand, but he wasn't one of them. He wore a shiny gun.

He stared at Jack, more surprised than worried.

Jack lifted his head an inch.

"I'm Davy Bates," the kid said.

The name stirred up lost memories in Jack, but he dammed them back. This country had taught him to be cautious, reserved. It made him alert and suspicious, a holding back against the appearances that too many times turned false or disappointing, or sometimes dangerous. The rawness of the country fed the New England core of his roots, the wait-and-see rule. The test. Out here, anyone could claim to be someone else. Maybe the kid was just looking to make a reputation by taking on Jack Tyson. But the other part of Jack wanted to admit that, yes, this was Davy Bates, he looked close enough right off. He was tempted to be friendly: why not step out fast and bring the boy in right away? But, no, Jack couldn't do that. He had not seen the real Davy since he was about twelve years old. This was probably Davy Bates just as the unsure kid said he was—but more important, maybe he wasn't.

"Are you Jack Tyson?" the kid asked, leaning forward, anticipating the steady-eyed man at the door.

A fly buzzed loud on the porch.

"Davy Bates?" the kid repeated, turning it to a question this time.

"I know the name," Jack said, and stepped to the edge of the porch, the first sign of acceptance and beginning trust. The kid had no way of knowing the full meaning of what his name had recalled in Jack—a primordial flush in his gut of family link and security.

The fly buzzed into the cabin.

Davy smiled, but he waited for the confirmation. He leaned toward Jack for the answer, hung between hope and disappointment.

"Yeah, I'm Jack."

Davy's smile spread all the way back. He took off his hat and rubbed his forearm across his pale forehead, half to wipe the sweat, half to say he had finally done it. "I've been looking for you for months. Colorado, Arizona, Kansas."

"I've been there," Jack said, now recognizing the shape of the nose, and the cut of the eyes and mouth, the vertical mold of the head.

"I'm your sister's son."

"Yeah, I know."

"I've been looking all over the place for you," he said, jubilant, swinging his arm across the horizon, looking at the high desert plains and the vast waves of dry terrain and shallow arroyos. "I'd get word of you, and by the time I got there, you were gone. Then I got someone who said he thought you went north, so I rode up there, but somebody there said you were here in Caliente. So I kept on riding."

"Come on," Jack said, seeing the same barn-brown color in Davy's hair as in Jessica's. His sister was always more steady than he was—always talking more, dreaming more, constantly working the farm even as a kid. She used to keep her hair long and tied back with colored ribbon she changed every day. Jack teased her about it and she said, quick as a whip, that every day was different so why shouldn't her ribbon be too.

Davy put his hat back on, swung off, led his horse to the cabin, and tied her up.

A quickness had filled the kid's body from the exhilaration of finding his uncle. The blood link had ignited a tie of safety, as if the indebtedness of being a relative were irrevocable.

Davy glanced around the cabin. "It's cool in here," he said, smiling. "It feels good, real good." But it was plain that the good feeling was finding Jack.

The cabin was swept clean and kept sparse—a cord bed, an eating table, two chairs, planks to hold water pots for washing and cooking, a grill over ashes on a flat-stone hearth, a stock of kindling and firewood, towels, tin plates and bowl, not much else.

Davy kept smiling and moving his arms and shifting on his feet. "I didn't think this country was so big out here," he said. "I mean, I rode for days and days to get anywhere. And then I was nowhere. I about died of thirst down out of Hot Rock. No rivers, nothing. And some people I wasn't going to ask anything. You can tell just looking at them that they're not about to give you two words or anything. So I lost a lot of time just not knowing anything about out here.

"In Arizona, I almost got drowned by some flash flood. I heard about them back home, but I just couldn't keep thinking about flash floods all the time. One day I heard this big roar, and I didn't know what was going on. It sounded like thunder, but there was nothing, no clouds, nothing. I was going to cross some dry bed, and my horse went rearing up. Then this huge wall of water came rushing down that dry bed. I couldn't believe it. It just plowed right through. I could've been plowed under with it. That was something."

Jack listened from the back wall. When Davy mentioned the words "back home," Jack pictured the New Hampshire farm with brooks and thick forests and stone walls around cleared fields. Where he lived now was a different world, almost beyond comparison. But the other world on the east side of the Platte and Missouri rivers was his footing, where he grew into what he was. New Hampshire was a tight roll of isolated valleys and notches, and families there were tough and wary, because they had to be. Independent and self-sufficient, because nobody wanted much to trudge up and over those endless valleys for the fun of it. That world made him economical, but he was seeing that Davy wasn't like that. The kid was spending words fast and not paying attention to anything else. Jack ladled a cup of water and handed it over.

"Thanks," Davy said, and smiled. He gulped it down, bending his neck full back, exposing it. He stood with his back to the open door; the sun outside framed him like a painting.

Jack watched the dangerous innocence Davy immersed himself in. The kid couldn't talk and still keep half his attention alerted to what was going on around him, where he stood, how he stood. He didn't know enough to stand against a wall where he could see in front of him and not have to worry about what was behind. He saw how Davy tilted his head all the way to drink the water and how he looked at the ceiling instead of Jack, or anybody else handing him water or whiskey.

Davy made a satisfying sigh and set the cup down on the table. "That makes you my uncle, doesn't it? Being the son of your sister."

"I guess it does."

"How long have you been out here?"

"I don't keep track. Five or six years."

"My mother says you've been out here forever."

"She's about right. Five years here is ten or twenty back there."

Davy smiled, showing his young teeth, apparently liking that thought. "She says you probably are some cattle king by now."

Jack smiled; that was like Jessica. He remembered how she was always planning to have the largest farm in the state.

First, she'd take over the family farm when their parents got too old to run it. After that she'd marry herself a strong husband and they'd make the land prosper, and buy adjoining acres, enlarge the prospects. Or she'd buy a bigger farm with good bottomland to start with and plant grain, which could lead to dairy farming. The country itself was growing, and that meant more people needed more milk and cheese and butter. She'd take on hired help and then buy up some more acres, just like climbing stairs to the top, she used to say. She'd have sons and they'd work the farm bigger too. Only it didn't work out that way.

Then in the sudden crack of his reverie Jack spotted someone who probably had trailed Davy on the sly. At instant sight Jack's insides gripped against his instinct to move survival fast, draw, drop down, and fire for his life—but now he recognized the man and let him be. Davy was so wound up that he missed seeing Jack's muted reaction, and didn't hear or sense the ambusher behind him at the bottom of the three plank-board steps to the porch.

The man smiled at Jack and then stepped, cougarlike, up the stairs without a sound.

CHAPTER 2

JACK kept his eyes on Davy, but his peripheral vision picked up the man sneaking around behind the kid.

"I'm not the same man my sister knew years ago," Jack said.

"You're still Jack Tyson," Davy went on, "no matter what. You can't change that much in five years."

"Out here you can."

The ambusher stepped silently to the door frame and stopped cold behind the kid.

"You probably want to know why I'm here," Davy said. "Why I tracked you down."

"You'll tell me when you want to."

"I might as well now."

Jack waited. He stood upright and straight now, leaning only slightly against the back wall, his thumbs hooked in his front denim pockets. When Davy said nothing, he moved his fingers to say, Go ahead, tell him—as if this were the permission Davy needed.

The man behind Davy blocked the sunlight on the right side of the kid, but the shadow didn't cast far enough to enter the room.

"You know there are two of us," Davy said, turning the words into a hesitant question with his eyes. "I have a brother—Sam."

"I know."

"He's my younger brother."

Jack nodded.

"He's been working the farm with me ever since Dad died. It's a two-man farm and Mom can't do the heavy stuff, and there's a lot of that. Besides, she has to do the cooking and cleaning."

Out the corner of his eye, Jack saw the black-coated man behind Davy draw his gun in slow motion, easing it from the leather—all the time smiling straight at Jack, making sure it was all right with Jack, who could stop it if he wanted.

"Sam was always late doing this and doing that," the kid continued, "and I could never get him to do the chores that needed to be done when they needed to be done. And Mom couldn't either. He kept hanging around a bad crowd in town and getting more and more lazy and stirring up trouble just for the excitement of it, that's all. He wasn't really bad or anything. He just didn't like working the farm. Sure, it's hard work."

With the gun out of his holster, the ambusher smiled at Jack. Then he pointed the Colt .45 Peacemaker down at the plank-wood porch. He waited until Davy stopped talking and for Jack to say something.

Only, Jack didn't.

Then the man filled the silence with the unmistakable menacing click of cocking the trigger.

Davy jerked his head over his shoulder, his eyes white, nostrils flared, his back still broad as a bull's-eye.

"Bang, bang, you're dead," the man said, grinning, glancing past Davy to Jack across the room, the telltale joke in his eyes. "You're deader than skull and bones, friend. You're deader than last night's dream, and that, my adventurous youth, is what life is all about."

Davy stared at the grinning, shaved, deep-eyed, sweatless man, the one who told him in Caliente where Jack lived. The idea that he could have just been shot in the back shook his nerves, frightened him to the core, froze his eyes in terror.

"That's right, it's me again, kid. You're wondering how I did it, how I could follow you without your knowing. And in all this open country? How I could get the drop on you, pull the deadly trigger at point-blank range right four square on your back? Tell him, Jack, tell the youth from afar how I did it." He stuffed his .45 into the holster.

Jack only smiled.

"I'd tell him myself," he said, "but modesty does prevent me."

"This is Doc," Jack said, ladling out a cup of water and holding it out for his friend.

Davy could say nothing. Too much damage to his nerves.

Doc stepped through the doorway, took the cup of water, raised it high in unspoken toast, and downed it. The flap of his black jacket swung back partially. He was shorter than both Jack and Davy, but the sharp glint in his eyes seemed to enlarge his stance. His trimmed hair was black as his coat, his pants dusty desert-colored. He drank with his eyes on Davy's.

"You'll get used to Doc," Jack said. "He's OK."

"You didn't tell me you were a doctor when I met you in town," Davy said, finally beginning to recover his nerves.

"Oh, I'm not a real doctor. They call me Doc because I am something of a philosopher; I tend the ills of the intellect instead of the body. Did you go to school, Davy? Are you a literate young man?"

"I went to school," Davy said, not sure how to take the question.

"Well, always remember that it's what you put in your mind that counts. That's the difference between savages and *savants*."

"What's a man like you doing out west?"

Jack raised his head slightly and said, "There are some questions you don't ask a man out here, Davy. Some questions can get you killed."

"I only asked why he was out here."

Doc stepped closer, put his arm around Davy's shoulder, and said, "My friend, I like you. You've come to the right place. We're going to teach you which questions to ask and then we're going to teach you to not get killed. Or is it the other way around?"

Doc glanced at Jack across the close room, silently seeking permission for what he had already said to Jack's sister's son—a sign that the line of power between the two men had a history to it.

When Davy regained his balance, he told Jack how one day his brother Sam packed up and left the farm. Never said anything to Jessica except that he was going west. Said he hated farming. Farming was nothing but digging up granite boulders in spring and picking stones in fall. It was dirt work, dirt prison. He wanted to be on his own, not chained to a horse plow all his life. It was slow death, and not for him. He was going to make something of himself faster than farm chains let him.

Sure, farming was hard work, Davy said, and maybe that was the reason farmers were closing down left and right and moving out to where the soil was rich and deep and they didn't have to fight bedrock and boulders all the time. Men from New Hampshire were moving out in droves. From Vermont too, and Maine.

Only, Sam didn't leave to farm in the plains. Jessica knew that, and so did Davy. No, he was going to the cattle country he kept hearing about, past the Susquehanna and the Missouri, out where family wasn't watching him and telling him what to do. That was what he kept saying he wanted, to get out on his own.

So Davy and Jessica were left with the farm to run themselves. It couldn't be done. The northeast field didn't get plowed on time. The barn roof on the south side collapsed. Then one day Jessica heard about Sam through a friend of a friend who went west by the Union Pacific to sell tools. He said Sam was hanging around saloons and gambling for a living. Jessica was furious and told Davy she wanted Sam back to help with the farm. Either he came back to help Davy and her, or she was going to write him out of the inheritance.

Then, Davy saids, she started to cry, because that wasn't the real reason, about the farm. She grabbed Davy's arm and said that Sam was ruining his life, ruining his future. Word was, he was turning into a saloon gambler, a cheap card-player, making the wrong kind of friends. It wasn't right. It would lead to worse. The wrong kind would tempt him deeper into the wrong life. Hanging around saloons was dangerous for a boy like Sam, away from home like that, in the West.

The pleading tears and desperation in her voice were something that Davy hadn't seen in his mother before. The way she clutched his arm. The tears pouring from her. It did something to him, frightened him. Go find Sam, she said, please find him and bring him back. Save his life, she said. Don't worry about her, she'd get along. She'd hire a hand to help with the farm. Just find Sam.

Then she told Davy to look up his uncle Jack first. Jack was in New Mexico the last time he wrote her. Ask Jack, Jessica said—he'll help you find Sam. He'll know what to do.

"I said I'd try," Davy ended, and shrugged.

Silence reigned awhile as the three men avoided each other's eyes. Doc was the one who broke it. "Well," he said, bobbing his head side to side, "we all have our tales of tragedy, don't we, Davy? Runaway siblings, incensed mothers, brother against brother. It's Cain and Abel all over again. The trouble is, who's Cain and who's Abel."

"What's that supposed to mean?" Davy asked.

Jack leaned back against the wall. "Don't let him get to you."

"Davy won't let me get to him. He's come all the way out here to the dirt-grubbing savages in their savage country to save his wayward brother Sam."

"This isn't a joke," Davy said, his voice suddenly hard, eyes mixing anger and confusion.

"Davy, what if Jack here doesn't want to help you find long-lost Sam? What will you do then?"

"Then I'll find him myself," Davy said without hesitation, looking at Jack. "I'll find him myself."

"Are you forgetting how close you came to being shot in the back at point-blank range? It says something about your preparation, doesn't it?" Doc said, shaking his head, pursing his lips in mock concern.

"I know what I'm doing." A flash of fire in Davy's eyes spread to his neck and face. His jaw clamped hard against itself, and the bones in his cheeks shifted back and forth.

Jack knew what Doc was doing, and he didn't want it to get out of hand. Doc had a talent for pushing too far. So Jack shifted his feet and leaned back against the wall again. The move was slow and smooth, drawing attention to him the way a calm, steady-eyed man can do when he wants someone else to change tack or stop the threat. "Where'd you hear Sam was last?" he asked Davy.

Davy broke his look from Doc and said, "Here in New Mexico." The tightness faded.

"When was that?"

"Last year practically."

"So he could be anywhere," Doc interjected. Then as if all that was said and done before about Davy were meaningless, he looked straight at Jack and added, "But the more pressing question is, where are the Korpecs?"

The Korpec name quieted the room, and the quiet spread from Jack alone.

CHAPTER 3

TEN minutes later, the three men were in the saddle. Jack knew that Davy had no idea what was going on, but it had been the kid's decision to travel along with Doc and him. As they rode, Doc told Davy about what happened two years ago in Bonito, Colorado.

The Korpec brothers and their sister set up a bank. The sister waited until the customers were gone, went up to the teller, and pulled a gun. Her brother Ned at the door slipped inside and pulled a gun on the banker behind a side desk. Maggie shouted for the money—stuff it in the bag! The teller did it. She grabbed the sack and ran for the door. Ned was outside already. Max was holding the horses.

Then Maggie whirled around at the door and fired two shots inside. Ned was on his horse and shouting for Maggie to hurry up, to get out of there. She whirled back around, hit the door frame, and dropped the sack. The brothers were shouting to get out of there.

That's when Jack got in the way. He came out of the general store next door at the sound of the shots. Maggie raised her gun. Jack drew and fired. The shot bolted Maggie back against the bank door like a sledgehammer. She was dead before she hit the wood.

The brothers fired at Jack, but their horses turned the shots wild. Jack ducked into the general store and fired from the door, but the brothers cleared out.

A posse was formed, but they found nothing and lost their anger fast. The money was back in the bank, and that was enough.

Word got back to Jack that the Korpecs were after him for

killing their sister. They let it be known that any woman of his was fair game.

"Even my mother?" Davy asked, glancing at Jack riding to the side, letting the horses walk easy under the hot sun and glaring white terrain.

"If they found out that Jack had a sister," Doc said, "sure. We're not dealing with schoolboys, Davy. The Korpec brothers are ruthless. If they found out about Jessica, they'd get back to her and kill her."

Davy stared white-eyed at him.

"Jack knows that. Don't you?"

Jack turned to Doc and said nothing. His silence meant yes, he knew that.

"But Jack has someone else on his mind right now," Doc said to Davy.

"Who?"

Doc ignored the question, something that he would do only if it meant trespassing uncertain country. He looked at Davy with eyes that said, Forget it; stay away from it; now's not the time. The message was unmistakable. It was clear, too, that Doc knew what part of Jack's world not to enter, only to circle around.

They fell silent as they rode across a dry creek and up and over its far bank, the horses kicking sand and loose earth as they strained quick up the slope.

Jack carried the killing scars, and Doc knew it. Sure, Maggie Korpec leveled that .45 at him at point-blank range. Another second and she would have blown his heart out. And sure, she killed other men and it didn't show that she cared much because she was a second off in killing Jack. But a man didn't kill a woman—ever. That was the core of it. He could rope her, shove her, maybe slap her or worse, but killing a woman was beyond it all. The people who knew that Jack shot Maggie knew it from a distance. They weren't there up close. They had their say and they said it, but in the end this meant nothing to him. What mattered was what he said to himself.

Doc stayed away from the subject, out loud anyway. The two of them knew those scars were there, and it didn't take words to think about them. Maggie's death also meant that Jack and Doc took seriously what the Korpecs said about their turn, about what they'd do to any woman in his life.

Davy didn't hear this in the silence. Instead, he hungered for more words. "Did it happen that way?" he asked Jack finally.

"Is the kid calling me a liar?" Doc said first, smiling, keeping it light, out front fast so Jack wouldn't have to explain it. "I tell him the unvarnished truth, and he calls me a liar. Can you believe that, Jack? Can you stomach the gall of this easterner calling me a liar? Isn't truth fiction enough?"

"I'm not calling you a liar," Davy said, defensive, heading straight into Doc's trap. "I was just wondering if that's the way it happened."

"It seems to me that's the same thing."

"You're twisting it all up."

"Yeah," Jack said, "it happened that way."

Doc glanced at Davy and smiled the teasing triumph.

More silence. And then Davy asked, "How do you know the Korpecs are in town?"

"Because Jack has friends," Doc said. "Because a friend caught word that Ned Korpec and one of his cronies were in a cattle camp outside town and talking up a killing, talking about Maggie, about how they were going to get the man who did it. They were asking about Jack, all right. So I rode out here."

"How'd you know I wasn't one of them? I was asking about Jack, and you told me where to find him."

Doc laughed. "When you came swinging through those doors, I'd just heard about that crony of the Korpecs and how he was slithering around town asking slimy questions about Jack. So I asked you a question instead. You remember."

Davy just waited when Doc glanced at him with that oblique, stabbing grin on his face.

"Remember that? I asked you where you were from, and you said New Hampshire. So I knew."

"Knew what?"

"I knew you weren't with the Korpecs."

"No, you didn't."

"Davy boy, nobody says he's from New Hampshire, even if he's from New Hampshire. He says he's coming in from Ellsworth or Dodge City or Newton or Abilene or Hay City."

"I could have been lying."

"No, your eyes didn't have it in them anyway."

"Why did you follow me, then? I didn't tell you who I was."

"For the fun of it. Besides, I was riding out to tell Jack about Korpec anyway."

They rode in silence again. "Don't let him get to you," Jack said finally. The way he said it without any telltale threat in his voice, the way the calm of his voice fit the calm in his eyes, counteracted the rising jangle in Davy's nerves. Jack made the kid stop the baiting spiral that Doc was spinning Davy on. It was the slow turn of Jack's head, the faint, friendly stretch of a smile, the simple words that reassured Davy. The same reassuring, solid way Jack sat in the saddle and moved with the horse and country.

Then, lifting his head a little to urge Davy on, Jack said, "Why don't you ask him where he's from?"

"Yeah," Davy said, taking up the challenge, as if he thought of it himself, "so where are you from?"

"Caliente," Doc said, and grinned wide and white.

Davy couldn't help smiling back. "You know what I mean."

"Oh, you mean where I came from before that. Now that requires a long, involved answer, and I'm not sure we have time to discuss it. I'd have to trace my comings and goings from one town to the next, all along those cattle trails, then back and forth to Cheyenne and down there to Pueblo and all the way down to Concho, then over to El Paso, up to Tularosa. You'd get bored, Davy boy."

Jack turned and said, "He's from Massachusetts."

Davy smiled.

"He was a teacher."

"That figures," Davy said, grinning, trying to put the ridicule back on Doc.

"Of course I was a teacher," Doc said. "You don't think everyone that comes out here is a farmer looking for better dirt or running out on his bills, do you? I plow minds, Davy boy, not fields. The whole world is my school. I plow the furrows of this unkempt frontier, and it is the likes of me that will save this unbuttoned, slovenly country."

"He plowed a few girl students in Massachusetts," Jack said, smiling. "That's why he's here."

"How these stories spread I'll never know," Doc said, and dismissed them with a wave of his hand. "Lies, all of them."

Davy was smiling wide.

Caliente was a two-street town. Most of the wood-slat buildings were clustered together on the main street, but as people came and stayed, the new buildings—mostly houses—held their own separate spaces on the outskirts. Jeff's Outfitter Store had the biggest floor space of any business in town, and did the most everyday, ordinary trade. Molly's Restaurant next door served any meal at any time. Guy's Grocery Store, The Boot and Gun Shop, The Caliente Hotel finished out the row where a boardwalk linked them together.

The town was too small for a sheriff and police, newspaper, or bank, too raw for a church. People kept their own news, money, and God. When cowboys came through on a herd run and life got cheap, the men in town took it on themselves to set it straight, when they could. Otherwise, they left the shooting and fights and sporting women to take care of themselves. A killing got a posse together, but only as far as a half-day ride so they could get back before sundown.

The only exception was the time a cowboy accidentally killed a young boy in a drunken gunfight with the herd boss. The desperation of the nine families in town boiled into outrage. Children were the seeds of the town, and enough of them were growing up to have a school. Losing one to a drunken fight was like declaring war against the whole outside world. The men had to hold back two blazing-crazy women from riding with them. The men outrode the cowboy, caught him the next morning with no lynching trees around, tied him up, blasted him with their rifles, and left him for the vultures.

Water was plentiful enough underground in town, and fed cottonwoods and willows around there. When the second street formed, the livery and blacksmith held the end ground on the west side. Orwin's Saloon and Dance Hall lasted about six months before Orwin sold all his finishings and rode out of town, never to be seen again. Jimmie's Wood was where firewood was stacked and sold. Drifters could get a hot bath and a beer next door. Some houses finished off the street.

On the main street, the Road's End Saloon got the most dollars in town. Hank ran it wide open for any gambling and drinking and women that came along. He served food in the back room; a Mexican cooked beans and rice and enchiladas with hot chilis that burned out the gringos. Out front the mahogany bar, shipped from St. Louis, was the pride-and-joy furniture. The rest of the place was as rough-hewn as the rest of the dusty town—scratched mirrors, unpainted chairs, cracked windows. What the Road's End did for the town, which the people knew but didn't admit, was attract the wildness and bragging and gambling and drinking to one place. Sometimes the fighting and killing spilled out of the saloon and down the streets, and that was the danger for Caliente.

CHAPTER 4

THEY rode into Caliente from the southwest. Jack led the way on the back side of the first string of isolated houses. He kept his head straight when a back door slammed, ignoring the noise that turned Doc's and Davy's attention. A woman stood still near the low-built, whitewashed house and watched the three riders ease by, the wrong two men looking at her.

By the time they paralleled her, she had her hand at the base of her throat. "Jack?" she called, her voice tentative and unsure.

He didn't turn. He should have, but something in him kept him from it, as if he didn't want to acknowledge this show of fate.

She was a sturdy, light-haired woman wearing a blue-and-white everyday dress. The apron was for cleaning or baking or washing, whatever she was doing in the rear of the house. Her blue eyes were in demand by men in this country, but the way she stood and the sound of her voice were for Jack.

When he kept on riding, she called again, "Jack?" This time she walked down the path past a root cellar, a leaning wood pile, a utility tub in scraggly weeds, a garden with its green carrot tops, bean vines climbing a pyramid of poles, and spreading squash plants.

He stopped this time. He couldn't avoid it. He didn't want to stop; that was the reason he came this way. Jack was hoping she wouldn't see him riding behind the house instead of in front and down the beginnings of the street. Doc and Davy pulled reins behind him. Jack turned in the saddle, making the mellow creaking tones of worn leather as he did.

"Jack?" she repeated, approaching, wiping her hands on

19

the underside of the apron, looking at Davy, the one she didn't know. "Where are you going?" The words were a shadow of real meaning—why are you riding through back here, why aren't you stopping, why are you ignoring me?

"Hello, Linda," he said, glancing down the back row of wood-slat buildings to see if anybody was watching. Nobody was.

"I saw you out the back window."

"I'm glad you did."

"Hello, Linda," Doc said, touching the rim of his hat. "You're always good to see."

"This is Davy Bates," Jack said, motioning to the young stranger next to him. "My nephew."

"Pleased to meet you, ma'am."

Linda smiled for the introduction, but the heart of it returned to Jack. At a different time she would have asked where Davy was from, how long he was planning to stay. Instead, she asked Jack, "Is something wrong?"

He shook his head and glanced again down the row of buildings. But she knew him enough to know that something was wrong. He wasn't good at hiding it, not from her.

He wasn't good at hiding anything from women. Even when he was a kid, Jessica could always tell when he lied about stealing maple sugar chunks from the larder or when he went riding alone along the Ashuelot River when he was supposed to be baling hay.

Doc picked it up. "We're just going to show Davy boy here a little of the town," he said. "That's just about it. Maybe buy him a drink."

That was her opening. "I've got something here," she said. "Why don't you all come in?"

"How about later?" Jack said, smiling. "Maybe if you stay inside there, we'll stop on the way out." He tried to make it sound offhand and casual, as Doc would, but that kind of meandering, detouring talk wasn't in him. He shouldn't have said "stay inside."

"Something's wrong, isn't there?" she asked, looking up at Jack and squinting at the high sun behind him, saying the words that had already shown in her eyes.

He shook his head again, but it wasn't convincing. "It's hot out here, Linda. Maybe you better get inside for a while. Keep out of the sun."

When Jack moved his roan on, Doc and Davy followed. As they passed her, Doc looked over his shoulder, smiled, and said, "Something cool to drink sounds good to me. We'll stop by for sure."

Then Jack looked back at her and saw it on her face. She knew Doc only meant for her to get back in the house and stay busy, fix something up, keep out of sight.

When they turned between the hotel and livery toward the main street, Jack said, "I'll go in alone."

"You want him to stay back here?" Doc asked, motioning to Davy.

"I don't want him hurt."

"I can take care of myself, you know," Davy said, full of youthful bluster.

"Stay with Doc," Jack said. His voice had a sudden commanding timbre to it that doused the defensive flare in Davy's face. The kid got the message. "Do what he says."

"We'll be in later," Doc said.

Jack nodded and moved his roan nice and easy the rest of the way to the street and turned east. At the Road's End he dismounted, hitched the horse to the rail, and stepped up the two stairs to the boardwalk. Two men came out of Jeff's Outfitter Store with new shovels and axes and clanked them into the bottom of their buckboard. Two other men were sitting on a plank-wood bench and talking under the ramada in front of Molly's Restaurant.

He looked over the swinging doors a moment before pushing them in, to see who was inside, to adjust his eyes to the darkness.

A Mexican man and woman sat at a round table in the back left. Their plates were empty; they were finishing beer. The man was leaning his forearms on the table. The woman sat back in the spoke chair.

Hank stood leaning against the long shelf of bottles and talking to the other man inside.

Jack walked in at an angle from the door and glanced at both front sides of the room; no one was there. The swinging door squeaked to a stop.

The stranger at the bar twisted a little to look over his shoulder and watch Jack creak the floorboards to the other end of the bar.

When Hank greeted him with a simple "Jack," the stranger smiled, his scraggly face loose at the bottom but calculating at the top. He was dusty and sweaty; his red-brown hair hung in thick, neck-long, oily ropes. He was twenty, maybe twenty-one. The front pocket of his green-plaid shirt was ripped halfway down one of the side seams, and drooped over itself. His nose was broken once and healed out of sync with the rest of his face. No beard grew where a three-angle scar had ripped his right cheek. Despite it all, he had the makings of a good-looking young man. The rest of his face was healthy-looking. His teeth were straight and white.

The Mexicans watched Jack too, and then went back to their beer.

"Hank," Jack said in return, looking at the young stranger again and back at the bartender. "How about a whiskey?"

"Right up," Hank said. He grabbed a squat glass, rubbed a towel in it, poured the drink, and placed it on the glistening bar, the only wood in the room that shined. He was a barrel-bellied man, too much beer and beans and standing around. "You heard about the new trail herd camping at The Forks?"

"I heard."

"This friend here," Hank said, pointing his thumb at the man watching and listening, "been out there. Big herd, he says. Red, isn't it?"

"Red Meredith," the man said, the same loose smile and figuring eyes changing his face. He shifted his stance, facing Jack but this time leaning his left forearm on the bar, his glass in his right hand. He said his name with that hard, clear thrust of someone who expected strangers to know it. "Yeah, I seen it. Been out there. Maybe five, six thousand head. Coming up through central Texas."

"You working it?" Jack asked.

Red smiled and shook his head. "You Jack Tyson?"

Jack nodded.

Red kept his white-teeth smile going and said, "Maybe you can get yourself some bean money out there yourself."

"Maybe."

Red raised his glass and finished it off, his eyes still on Jack as he drank. He wiped his mouth with the back of his right hand, the glass still in it, his eyes still on Jack. Then he set the glass on the bar and said, "I'd buy you a drink, but you haven't finished yours yet."

"When I'm ready."

Doc and Davy walked in. The three men at the bar, and the Mexicans at the table, turned and watched them stop inside the doors and look around at the thick-air, shadowy saloon. They saw Davy stare at Red in recognition. They also saw that he was too wide-eyed and tight to be anything but green and untested. He stayed too close to Doc, and he kept looking at Jack.

Doc waved to Hank in his usual extravagant way and said,, "I'm buying a deck, Hank, and I'm going to show Davy here some rudiments of a game or two, some seven-up, some monte, all the important tools of earning a man a living." He pointed Davy to the table at the right front of the room. "Take that one over there." Then he walked to the bar between Jack and Red and slapped down a silver dollar. Hank grinned and slapped down a deck of cards to balance off the routine.

"Teaching the kid to be a man, huh?" Red said, grinning.

"That's me, all right," Doc said, picking up the deck. "Teacher of the card-game trade. Come on, try your luck."

"I'm drinking here with Jack Tyson. Besides, I ain't much for teachers."

"Not friendly," Doc said, grinning, shaking his head, "not friendly."

Red turned to Davy, already at the table. "Oh, I been friendly to that Davy there, wasn't I, kid? We met." He chuckled, making it obvious how he was the one who gave Davy a hard time earlier. "He's from New Hampshire, he tell you that?"

"Well, we're all from somewhere," Doc said. He walked to the table, sat down, and opened the deck. "Hank? We could use some half-bottle you got open, will you? Something from Kentucky charcoal, and two glasses."

"Coming up," Hank said, and grabbed the neck of a whiskey behind him. He walked around the end of the bar and took the bottle to the front table. "But I can't guarantee the charcoal."

"Yeah, I know," Doc said, laughing, looking at the bottle label. "I see you can't guarantee the Kentucky either."

"Hell no, but it's better than cactus juice."

Doc laughed, filled the two glasses, and shuffled the deck. He flipped his coat flap free of his holster. When Hank went back to the bar, Davy reached for his glass. But Doc pressed Davy's wrist down and shook his head once, his piercing eyes deadly serious and not to be tampered with. Davy did exactly as he was told.

"You sure, friend?" Doc called across the room. He held up the cards, his tone belying what was really going on.

"I said I was drinking with big Jack Tyson here," Red said, and pushed the glass toward the back of the bar for Hank to fill it again. "They know Jack Tyson where I come from."

"They do, do they?" Doc said, shuffling again. "They know him around here too. I guess he's famous. You famous, Jack?"

He shook his head. "Not that I know of."

"So you see, friend," Doc said, "he's not famous at all."

"Red Meredith."

"Well, Red Meredith, you must be mistaken. Jack isn't famous at all."

"I ain't mistaken. Jack Tyson killed a friend of mine. In fact, Jack Tyson shot down a woman—a goddamn woman. Maybe that's all he can do—shoot a goddamn woman."

Then Red Meredith turned to Jack.

Hank raised his hands and patted the air. "Now, come on, I don't want any shooting in here. No guns, you hear? No guns."

The Mexican couple stared at the scene. Then the man said to the woman in a tone higher than a whisper, loud enough for everyone to hear but low enough to not startle: *"Vamos."* They slowly slid their chairs back and stood up slowly, nothing fast and startlingly, nothing deceptive, nothing threatening. The man led the way to the door, the woman following close alongside the wall and then along the left front on the far side of the room away from Doc and Davy, and out the door, gone.

Hank reached slowly for a bottle behind him. "Here, have one on me. Both of you." But when the two men ignored him, he himself edged to the side, slowly.

"They tell me you shoot goddamn women," Meredith said.

"Now, Red," Doc said.

"You stay out of it," he shouted back, eyes fixed on Jack. He sniffed and grinned. "That right? You shoot goddamn women? You shoot Ned's sister? You shoot Maggie?"

"Maybe."

"You goddamn did."

"You weren't there."

"They told me. They told me what goddamn happened. You killed her. They saw it."

"She had a gun on me."

"You shot her in the back."

Jack shook his head, but he knew what was coming. A tautness filled his insides, a high-sprung alertness that seemed to overcome him against his own will, as if he were transformed to another sphere of survival and stubbornness. He would not—could not—let go and turn away. Not now. Not when this kid Meredith faced him with the Maggie killing. But Meredith saw only the cat-calm exterior. He missed the deadly calm inside Jack, and that was Meredith's critical mistake.

"You shot her in the goddamn back. They saw it. They told me about it."

"You got it wrong, Red."

"Now I'm going to kill you in the gut, the front gut. Me, Red Meredith."

All the time Jack half leaned on the bar. He let the man simmer to a boil and waited for the heat to push his nerves to the bursting point. "It didn't happen that way, Red."

"Red Meredith. Say it."

"She had a gun on me."

"Say it."

"It wasn't the way they told you, Red."

"Red Meredith, Red Meredith!"

The shout of his own name unleashed the man's instincts. The pressure cock released the coiled spring in his twitching right hand.

The two men caught each other's surge of power in the minuscule movement of fingers and hands and eyes.

Meredith went for his gun.

Jack whirled around full front, grabbing and freeing his Colt from his holster.

Then another power split the room.

A pistol barrel and hand stuck over the swinging doors. Straight at Jack.

In milliseconds Doc clamped his left hand on Davy's chest and shoved him full force back, tumbling him over the chair and onto the floor, crashing and breaking the chair, too fast for Davy to say anything.

With his right hand, Doc pulled his .45 and fired at the ambusher. The blast thundered through the room. The slug splintered the far doorjamb.

The ambusher fired a lightning moment later, but his aim was destroyed. The fraction of an inch wrong made the difference. The slug shattered a bottle behind the bar, the splattering glass shards making the exploded liquid suddenly loud and destructive.

Jack squatted to the floor and stretched his arm.

Red Meredith fired chest high, a dead man's hope—a death-grip reflex that pulled the trigger. Jack's bullet had whammed upward into the twenty-year-old heart and jolted Meredith's body into an ugly backward convulsion, slamming his torso into a visible version of the huge explosion of the Peacemaker—a dead-puppet fling of arms and legs, until it landed deadweight, a gunnysack thump on the dirty plank-wood floor.

An instinctive moment later, Jack sprang to his feet and ran after Doc through the swinging doors.

Doc pointed to the man running behind Jeff's Outfitter Store.

Ned Korpec.

CHAPTER 5

JACK pointed Doc to the left side of the outfitter store while he ran across the street to the right. They reached the boardwalk at the same time, both of them stepping quietly but quickly to the corners of the building, their leveled guns in hand.

The shots at the Road's End had cleared the street. The men buying tools had sped out of town, their buckboard churning up dust. The two men talking under the ramada at Molly's Restaurant had disappeared inside someplace. Nobody had come out when shots cracked open the quiet. They stayed put inside to let the shooters settle it and not catch any stray slugs.

Except Davy. He pushed open the doors of the Road's End and stepped onto the boardwalk, bold and stupid. "Jack?" he called.

Doc turned around, and Jack swung his hand and arm backward, a short, hot, angry gesture. When Davy didn't move, he shouted, "Get back in there."

The heat in the words pushed Davy backward through the swinging doors. They also signaled Ned Korpec where Jack was.

Jack looked at Doc at the other corner of the building. He knew what Doc was thinking—it was a mistake to shout like that. He knew, too, that Davy was a sudden new presence in Jack's life that had to be reckoned with, that the kid could get killed like a dumb hare on a panic run. It didn't take much to exchange the same thought: Davy could be shouted back into the saloon out of harm's way, but it wouldn't take long for the kid to buck himself up and come out again, once the heat in Jack's voice had died out. Davy would have to take his chances, and Doc's look showed that he knew Jack now had to take his chances with Davy.

They waited on each other's savvy, but it was Jack who gave the motion, the slight back tilt of his head that said, Now!

Jack sprinted down the side of the building to the waist-high stack of desert-bleached lumber at the far end and crouched behind it. He waited, picturing in his mind the way Doc would run the same way in a sprinting crouch on the other side of the building until he came to something to shield him, an old propped-up door or a thrown-out tub or a pile of stones. Then Jack eased closer to the corner of the building and crouched to his knees, because if Korpec was there he'd expect a man after him to show himself standing up.

A second after he edged around the corner, Doc did the same. Nothing. Korpec was gone, probably scared off by the shout Jack gave at Davy.

Jack ran low to Doc. They studied the scene, the cluttered backside of the stores with the leftover rough-hewn building timbers and helter-skelter junk—broken chairs, ripped mattresses, frames without pictures or mirrors, sawhorses and heaps of fence posts. Korpec could be behind anything solid.

Jack pointed the barrel of his Peacemaker back down the side of the building to the main street and angled it to the right, clear enough to Doc that he was to go back to where he started and head down the front of Guy's Grocery Store, cutting Korpec off from crossing over to the Road's End side of town. Jack would stay on the backside and close in on Korpec from there, forcing him to move toward Doc, getting him caught in a crossfire.

Doc ran to the front of the outfitter's store. Jack waited and watched him until he disappeared around the edge of the building. Then he ran to the stack of firewood next to an abandoned buckboard. Some movement or glint of sunlight on a hinge or something caught his eye for a moment, making him think Korpec was behind an outhouse. But the man would have to be a plain idiot to get behind that; with no place to get other cover, he'd be good as dead, blasted apart from both sides.

Jack waited and listened. Nothing. He studied the path to a stack of adobe clay bricks. All clear, no potholes he could see, no roots. He steadied himself, then sprang into the open and ran the thirty feet to the bricks.

Halfway there Korpec stuck his gun above a back-door stoop and blasted a slug past Jack's head.

Jack lunged forward by the momentum of his run, hit the sand with his shoulder, and rolled over and over toward the bricks, the sand and dust puffing up as he rolled. Korpec's second shot splattered a brick into chunks and straw and a fine spray of dried clay. Jack stretched his arm around the side of the stack and fired. The bullet thudded and splintered the wood on the top step.

Korpec laid low while Jack had the line of sight to himself. It happened so fast that Doc wouldn't have had enough time to get to the second building where Korpec was. Jack couldn't do anything but wait. At the sound of the shots, Doc would come running down the gap between the outfitter and grocery stores, the wrong alley.

Korpec knew that the shots would draw Doc back from the main street. Jack saw the top of Korpec's head move as he crawled away from the stoop to stand-up protection of the far side of the building. It wasn't enough for a clear shot, a wasted shot.

When Doc reached the back, he crouched down at the corner of the outfitter's store and saw Jack waiting for him behind the bricks. Jack pointed fast that Korpec had run down the next alley. He signaled Doc to go back to where he was. No shouts, no words. Jack would be going down where Korpec ran. They could still get him in a crossfire.

Doc nodded toward the stoop. Jack readied himself by digging his boot into the dirt, pushed himself upright, and ran low and fast to the stoop. He skidded headfirst into the ground and propped himself tight against the meager barricade. Then he turned around and saw that Doc was covering him, just as he knew he would.

Without a nod, Doc ran back down the gap between the buildings to the main street.

Jack waited until he figured Doc would be at the front boardwalk. Then, with gun up, he crept around the stoop so his boots wouldn't creak the old wood. It was a risk. If Korpec was still there, Jack was a sitting duck, with no backup from Doc. Doc either had to ease down the front of the store to head Korpec off at the alley, or he would be an easy target if Korpec had already made it to the front and was setting up an ambush.

Jack eased into the full sight line of the alley, and the more straight-on view he had the tighter his inner coil grew. But Korpec was gone.

Then Jack ran between the buildings and stopped at the front right corner. Doc was waiting for him at the other side and slipped into the alley to get out of the way from wherever Korpec was hiding. Doc shrugged; he didn't know where the man was. Jack nodded across the street. Doc frowned and shook his head, knowing what Jack was going to do. When Jack nodded and motioned again toward the other side of the street to make it totally clear, Doc pursed his lips hard and shook his head again. Jack shrugged to say that this was the only way to draw Korpec out.

Doc acceded and set himself gun high and ready against the side of the building.

Jack tightened his jaw and eyes, waited for any movement on the street, took a deep breath, and sprinted into the open. He ran a snake course, fast and furious, his boots kicking dirt and dust. A second before Korpec fired, Jack tumbled on a shoulder-and-back roll, somersaulting back to his feet and weaving in and out of the line of fire.

Korpec's shot missed, and so did his second, but they showed where he was.

Doc crouched to his knees and fired off two split-second shots at Korpec behind a freestanding shed between the grocery store and The Boot and Gun Shop. He was on Doc's side of the street; he hadn't crossed over.

Jack dove behind a stack of grain sacks in front of the hotel.

Then came the kind of quirk that get men killed—the greenhorn interference that experienced men too often forget can happen. Davy pushed open the swinging doors of the Road's End Saloon and with his gun out shouted, "Jack, you all right?"

Doc turned at the same instant Jack did.

Korpec in a pressured panic reflex swung his gun to the left diagonal and fired at Davy, who was standing like a statue in broad daylight. The slug ripped into a post holding the sun roof, exploding the wood into a splintered gash two feet from Davy's heart. Davy jumped back into the saloon, but the damage was done, the timing shattered.

Korpec disappeared.

Jack signaled for Doc to get back to the rear of the buildings. Then he ran across the street and down the side of the building Korpec ran down. Three quarters of the way to the backside, he crouched behind a half-filled rain barrel and listened. Nothing. He waited to hear a shuffle of pebbles, the creak of a wood-slat porch, anything that sounded Korpec's location. But Korpec must have run fast all the way to the rear. The two buildings had no doors to the alley, and the windows were closed. Korpec could have climbed into a window and shut it, but that would have taken too long. It was too noisy, too risky.

No, Korpec had made it to the back. Jack moved to the side of the rain barrel to see the rest of the alley. The only obstruction was a stack of lumber airing alongside the building next to him; it was too low for Korpec to hide behind. It would be dangerous for Jack to try to make it to the rear of the building, because he'd be totally exposed in those last ten feet. Korpec could wait until Jack was midway and suddenly spring around the corner for the kill.

But Jack was counting on Doc to make it along the backside of the building. That would protect him enough. He waited another fifteen seconds, then bent low and moved with caution in his feet, his eyes steady on the edge of the building for the slightest movement or color that meant Korpec and his gun. He made no sound himself, nothing but the tightened breath from his lungs, the light, hunter press of his boots on the dust above the sun-packed earth.

He passed the stack of lumber, then neared the corner of the building where the light of the open country poured in and seemed to blare out his vulnerability. He kept his focus on the left edge of the building where the chances were good that Korpec would be. The closer he stepped, the more the right back side appeared. Then he stopped and waited, his ears brittle with alertness for the merest sound. Again, nothing.

With peripheral vision, he saw the familiar way Doc moved, the shape of his body, the black of his coat. He loosened up, feeling the assurance again that the next split second he wouldn't face Korpec's killing blast into his gut.

As slowly and gingerly as Jack did, Doc stepped over stones and patches of weeds. They glanced at each other and then in their soundless way moved into another phase of their trap, trying again for the crossfire, trying to draw Korpec out, using the simmering panic in the hunted one that would break his nerve and expose him.

Doc opened his free hand to tell Jack that he saw no sign of Korpec. Jack stepped to the edge of the building while Doc kept his slow-motion steps going. Now Jack could see the debris behind the next building—two broken barrels, a rusted long-handle shovel, a ladder lying on loose hay.

At first the shed with the half-open door looked too

convenient and obvious for Korpec. Doc shook his head too, then motioned toward the adobe foundation of an unfinished house. He swung his finger toward the shed, telling Jack that he'd move around the back of the shed to get a wider angle on the foundation. Jack could move in close by the buildings and get at the opposite angle.

Doc kept the same calculating catlike steps, avoiding anything that would snap into noise. He stepped closer to the shed and, when the shed created a blind spot on the foundation, he quick-stepped around it.

Jack crept close along the building. Nothing moved or sounded from either the shed or the foundation. Then he saw the back alcove doorway with a rain overhang. The door was set back in a darkened insert, deep enough to hide a man. But that was too vulnerable for Korpec to hold off the two of them. Still, Jack could see how tempting it would be. The doorway nagged at his attention. He fought against anticipating the glint of gunmetal sticking out, because anticipating false threats was self-destruction; he'd seen it happen to others. But the doorway pulled at his focus, adding another possibility to keep track of—the shed, the foundation, the doorway, the edge of the far building.

Then he saw the cracked window up ahead, and the idea of Korpec inside the building made sense. The killer could pick off Doc or Jack and never be seen, a clear view. The bright sun outside with the darkness of the inside was perfect.

Jack saw how Doc was moving into the angle of vision of the window, past the shed, a dead shot. Nothing protected him.

But it wasn't the window.

Korpec leaned over the skirting of the flat-top roof. He stretched his gun straight at Doc, angling the weapon downward for the close easy kill, the anger and snarl in his eyes and mouth.

The fragment of movement against the mammoth solidity

of the building caught Jack's eye—the metal shape of death, the trip wire of survival. The sprung instinct in him raised his hand without the slightest calculation, and his gun pointed Korpec to death. He fired three times in a thunderous explosion of bullets, the coagulated noise belying the bewildering swiftness of the shots. Which hot slug of lead hit Korpec in the bloody neck and broke through his skull didn't matter. It was probably the first, and enough from the tremendous shock to bolt the screamless corpse sideways over the corner roof skirting.

When Korpec fell in a twirl of dead arms and legs, only then in this split-second scene did Jack sense the smartness in the man, how he had climbed the ladder to the roof and pushed it down to the noiseless hay, how he waited for Doc to get in the killing clear. Smart.

CHAPTER 6

DAVY was the first to come out on the death-still main street when Jack and Doc walked from the outfitter's store alley, their guns holstered, their gait slow and casual. Then one by one the townspeople stepped into the doorways, sauntered their cautious way to the edge of the porches, leaned out open windows. The people seemed to make the buildings themselves loosen up and breathe in new vigor and life, as if those three hell-fire bursts of bullets from Jack's gun in the unseen distance was the scalpel that cut out an ugly tumor on the town.

Three men hurried down one of the alleys to see the dead Korpec and piece together what happened. They wouldn't be able to make clear sense of the scene until Jack and Doc told them the details, but that wouldn't stop the conjectures from spreading fast. Ned Korpec would be in the ground by sundown, probably sooner, and that word would ripple out of Caliente in every direction until his brother Max heard it.

But for now Davy was the only one who quick-stepped to Jack and Doc coming across the street toward the Road's End. The kid's eyes were filled with awe and fantasy. He had never seen anything like this; it was written all over his face. A hunt to the death, and Jack could have gotten killed, only he didn't. He won. He killed his killer.

The enthusiasm of fear showed in the kid's mouth, an ambivalent, scared smile that mixed relief with a gasp of reassurance that *he* was alive because Jack and Doc were alive, that Jack was right there in front of him, that Korpec was dead someplace in the back, it didn't matter where.

He ran up and put his hand on Jack's arm. "That was . . ."

he said, the bubbles of his youth straining to burst, "that was . . . amazing. I couldn't believe it. I heard those shots and I didn't know what was happening. I mean, I wasn't sure, I wasn't sure."

Jack and Doc kept walking straight ahead.

Davy got out of their way and skipped to Jack's side. "I saw you running right out in the open," he continued, his eyes still wide and admiring, his excitement hot and propelling, "and I didn't know what you were doing. But you had a plan, didn't you? I couldn't tell what it was. You were drawing him out—but it was dangerous, really dangerous. He could've shot you. He almost shot me. I just wanted to see if you were all right."

Jack turned to meet Davy's eyes and said nothing.

"I shouldn't have done that," he said, shaking his head, misinterpreting Jack's look. "I know I shouldn't have done that. It was really dumb, wasn't it? I know it was." Then Davy looked to Doc, who wasn't his talkative self.

When Jack looked to Doc, an unsaid understanding passed between them, but not to Davy. Jack grabbed Davy's arm, stopping him. "What?" Davy asked, glancing at Doc walking away.

"You see these," Jack said, holding out his hands.

Davy stared at Jack's upturned palms. "They're shaking," he said of the obvious. He looked up, disbelieving. "But how could you be doing that?"

"They're shaking now. Not then."

Davy watched Doc walk around the corner of the Road's End and disappear. "Where's he going?"

"Back there someplace."

"Why?"

"You see these?" Jack said, again holding his trembling hands out to Davy. "Men react different ways."

Davy stared at Jack, but his eyes were hollow because he couldn't fit the parts together the way he thought they should be. He asked, "What happens to Doc?"

Jack knew, but he didn't say. "Maybe he needs to be alone. Some men get sick and throw up. I've seen men go on a shooting rampage, emptying their guns on tree trunks. Some just get drunk. Doc'll be back. Come on."

He led Davy up the Road's End boardwalk and sat down on the slat-back bench. The people who made themselves seen kept their distance and stole their looks. It was a raw kind of etiquette that Davy didn't fathom.

Jack leaned on his knees, folded his fingers tight against the shaking, and fell silent. His eyes stayed alert on the street but not with the extreme distrust that might have come from another man. He knew the brash boy next to him was eager for talk and heroics, and was confused about not getting it. He turned to Davy and held out the flat of his hands again. "It's going," he said, showing the boy how his hands were still trembling, though not as much.

"But you won."

"I survived."

"I guess I'd be shaking too."

"I hope so."

Davy looked for what Jack meant.

"If you don't react somehow, you're dangerous to yourself. You'll think you're immortal and turn careless."

They fell silent again.

Doc walked around the corner and caught Jack's eye. Then he stepped up the stairs and leaned against a front post, facing the two of them, saying nothing while Davy just stared at him. Finally, he smiled and said, "Didn't expect to see me on two feet again, right, Davy boy?"

"No, I did," Davy countered right away, waiting for the talk to come. "I knew I would. Only, I did a dumb thing there, didn't I?"

"Did you tell him what a dumb thing he did?" Doc asked Jack, who shook his head. "Then I won't either."

"I could have got you both killed."

"Maybe."

"All I know is that I want to shoot like you," Davy said, looking at the two seasoned men that he, of all in the reawakened town, sat with in plain sight.

The words couldn't be dismissed as just another display of youthful exuberance. They came as an echo that sounded like Jack's own early years in this country, only this time they seemed unbelievably innocent and inexperienced to Jack. They could have come from his own mouth when he stopped in Abilene on his way west and saw a grizzled, dark-haired drifter in a gunfight make the second move and get the first shot. He remembered the excitement of seeing such controlled speed and deadly accuracy with a firearm. It impressed him beyond any sight he'd seen. Unlike Davy, he knew no one to tell he wished he could shoot like that, but he had thought it, and had felt the drive to do what he thought. Hearing those words from Davy now dredged up a disturbing memory.

Jack exchanged the same knowing thought as Doc when he glanced at him, but it was Doc who spoke first. "Davy boy," he said, "do you know what a man does? He gets a goal and he sticks to it. What'd you come out here for?"

"To see Jack."

"You know what you came out here for. You came out here to find Sam. Stick to it. Find Sam and take him home to New Hampshire."

Davy looked to Jack for support, and didn't get it. "But I like it here."

"Find Sam," Jack said.

"All right, I'll find Sam, but look at what happened today. I have to learn to use this"—he patted his Colt—"because I'll be alone." He waited for a response. "Well, won't I?"

"Don't look for trouble," Jack said.

"Trouble came in here," Davy said. "You didn't look for it. It tracked you down. Only you had Doc, and Doc had you. Who am I going to have? I have to have my gun."

"That's not your only alternative," Doc said, shifting on his feet, leaning his other shoulder against the post. "Use your *head* to stay out of trouble."

"Doc is right," Jack said. "Your mother needs you alive, not buried out here someplace."

"*You're* alive."

Jack glanced at Doc. Both of them knew what they were going to have to do. They saw it in each other's eyes. They just let it happen, they let Davy work up to it.

"Well, you are," Davy repeated, looking at each of them in turn with a challenge to deny it, just like an obvious-minded kid with a shiny gun would do.

"We're alive because we use our heads," Doc said.

"And your guns."

Jack sighed and leaned back on the bench. "Davy," he said, shaking his head and stopping, because he heard in his mind's ear the trap that his own life had made for the boy's convenience right here and now, the boy with Jack's blood line in his veins.

"Be a man, Davy boy," Doc said. "Do what you're supposed to do. Find Sam and go back home. Do your duty. Honor thy father and mother."

Then Davy said what Jack and Doc knew he would, and what they had agreed in silent exchange they would do. He said it as if this was the first time he thought of the idea, and maybe it was. "Will you help me find Sam? Both of you?"

They walked their horses to Guy's Grocery Store, hitched them, went inside, and stocked up—beans, dried beef, salt, pork fat, rice, coffee, hardtack, more of the usual. They came out and stuffed their saddlebags with the provisions, ready to leave in the morning. They'd sleep at Jack's cabin and be on their way before sunrise.

They got ready to mount up, and that was when Jack saw Linda.

She was hurrying down the street in the billowy dust, sometimes breaking into a little trot. She was there to see

Jack and nobody else. Twenty feet away from the three men, she stopped and fixed her eyes on the one who mattered the most.

Doc finished mounting up and said with a no-uncertain tone, "Come on, Davy." The two of them gave their horses wide berth around Linda because the way she had stopped away from them made it obvious that she wanted to be with Jack alone.

Jack took the reins, walked to the only woman who cared for him, and let Doc and Davy move away. He knew that Doc would tell the boy about Linda. He'd heard it before, how Linda's name meant "clear light." And that was what she was to Jack all right. It was a tease when Doc said it with that man-succumbs-to-woman smile in his eyes, but for Davy he'd go on to tell him about the grand truths the kid wouldn't understand. He'd tell Davy about the sex that Jack and Linda could give each other, and get a lusty grin out of the boy. Then he'd say something oblique about the loneliness of the country and that a woman like Linda made the desert green for the right man—brought some comfort and joy to a life that otherwise wasn't much more than opening one can of beans after another.

That was what a woman was out here, an oasis, a life-giving spring, another self found at last.

Doc would warn Davy to be careful what he said about Linda to Jack's face. Doc knew when to back off on Jack. He'd told Jack more than once that Linda was the one, go ahead and marry her once and for all. He'd told him time and again that she and Jack were ready for each other. But Jack was his own counsel, Doc would say: Keep that in mind, Davy.

Now Linda had worry in her eyes when Jack walked to her. He liked that, and he knew Doc was right about the two of them. The trouble was that this goddamn country made him more on his own than anywhere else in his life. Sometimes it outright forced him to be the way he didn't want. Sure, he wanted her, but at the same time he wanted—needed—the open gate that came with the West. He wasn't sure about it, not sure at all.

"You all right?" she asked, reaching to him and touching his chest as he closed the distance.

He nodded.

"I heard the shots. I was scared for you, Jack."

"It had to be done."

"I know. You're not hurt?"

"No."

The worry vanished, and her eyes softened. A glimmer of a smile appeared, a sign that knowing he was safe and with her had rebalanced her. The sudden softness said that she saw facets in him that no one else did. It was a mystery to Jack, but he liked it.

He turned, and together they walked down the main street. Doc and Davy were sauntering far in front of them. Davy, not Doc, was the one who had to turn in his saddle to see what was happening.

They walked silently past Molly's Restaurant and the hotel. Linda knew the signs. She saw the stuffed saddlebags and how the three of them had just come out of Guy's Groceries.

"When are you leaving?" she asked, looking straight ahead, her slow steps matching his.

Jack smiled at the knowing way she put it. "Sunrise."

"Because of what happened?"

"No, but it's not a bad idea to get away from here awhile. Davy's my nephew. He's just a kid, younger than he thinks he is. He's looking for his brother. My sister thinks Sam's up to no good and wants Davy to straighten him out."

"Does he know where Sam is?"

"No."

"So he wants you to help him."

"He's Jessica's son, Linda. My sister's boy. He's just a kid. I have to look after him or he'll get into trouble."

"What about Caliente? Everybody knows that Ned's

brother will be coming through here looking . . ." She didn't finish it.

"Looking for me."

She turned to him and said nothing.

"It'll be better if I'm not here."

"When will you be back?"

This time he said nothing.

They walked in silence the rest of the way. Doc and Davy had stopped at Linda's house and were waiting for them. Jack wanted to take her hand, but Davy was watching him and something rigid and commanding prevented him from simply reaching for her as she did to him. He had to wait until he got alone with her inside the house, behind the closed door, out of sight. Doc would make it happen and keep Davy outside with him. Then Jack would take Linda and kiss her hard.

CHAPTER 7

AT daybreak Jack and Doc had a cooking fire going, coffee bubbling, and oats that soaked overnight heated up before Davy cleared his eyes. Then before the first long shafts of sunrise broke over the straight-edge horizon, the three of them were in the saddle and heading north toward Santa Fe. They rode three abreast over the shallow, rolling terrain, the cool of the night lingering in the fresh morning air, the vast silence of the West engulfing them with almost feelable presence. The pungency of the sage had its own private presence as they rode through the small clumps, around the large ones, and the spindly tentacles of the ocotillo made the eye remind the head that this country was lean and sparse, a stark and plain place.

Silence held sway here at daybreak and sunrise. What a man could see and smell took second billing. True, the horses' hooves sounded mute in the sand and on the root-padded clay, their lungs bellowing out air through their flared nostrils, and the creak of saddle leather made an unfigurable rhythm. But it was the heavy silence that seemed to have mammoth dimensions in the early hours, almost visible in a conspiracy with the sunrise, because the more light that appeared over the horizon to the right the more solid and seeable rose the silence. Night had quieted the wind for the morning, and that, too, added power to what should affect only the ear, and not also the eye.

To Jack, this kind of morning kept making him what he was. Daybreak here turned the world to a quiet alertness, an open but cautious country intent on protecting other parts of itself. At the same time, the long sweeping vistas offered a peacefulness in the mornings, easy to get along with and friendly as it unfolded with the rising sun. This was what Jack claimed of it—a feeling of being part of the newness, of being among the few who traveled this land, fewer still who stayed.

They rode without speaking for the first few miles. The solid fire body of the sun finally arched over the edge, brightening the desert floor, obliterating the biggest stars. The butte cliffs turned red. The flat-topped mesas and isolated etched columns of hard-packed sandstone cast long shadows on the Southwest floor, but that wouldn't last long. When the sun set itself free of the horizon, that signaled the beginning of the real day, and what that fully meant.

Now and then Jack turned in his saddle and looked over his shoulder, as Doc did too, though not as frequently. Jack caught Davy's eye when he turned back around one time, but the kid didn't ask what his face was questioning. The whole force of the morning quiet and the unarticulated life around them suppressed the kid and made him like Jack and Doc.

But when Jack turned around the next time after they covered another mile, Davy couldn't help it. "What's wrong?" he asked, twisting his neck back too. The question had changed into worry.

Jack looked over to him. "Nothing."

"Then why are you doing that?"

Jack smiled a little. Before he glanced at Doc, he said, "To make sure nothing is wrong."

Doc laughed, and took it from there. "Remember, Davy boy, how you got shot in the back at Jack's cabin? I followed you all the way from town and not once, mind you, not once did you turn around. Of course, you probably wouldn't have seen anything anyway."

Davy smiled back.

"Ah, what we learn in life," Doc said, grinning, "if we live long enough. Go ahead, Jack, tell the kid what else."

Jack pointed straight ahead. "You see up ahead?" he asked, making Davy look at a breach in a dry creek, a series of wind-carved sandstone chunks, clusters of sage and creosote bushes.

"Yeah."

"The way they look now won't be the same when we get past them. If we have to turn around and go back for some reason, they'll look different. The right side will be left, everything reversed. The shadows will change. The colors too, because the sun will be at a different angle. So if you keep looking back once in a while, where you've been won't look so unfamiliar if you have to backtrack."

Davy was leaning on every word, as if Jack were spelling out a phenomenal insight, and to him it was. Suddenly, Jack was a brilliant teacher of a simple but profound wisdom. "Yeah," Davy said again, only this time it revealed an understanding of something that was right there in front of his very eyes, and it took Jack to show him.

They rode through the breach in the dry creek and back onto high ground. A half mile later Davy turned in his saddle and looked over his shoulder, all official-like as if he had done this by habit since he first arrived in the Southwest.

Jack and Doc smiled at each other.

They rode without a word for another half mile, but the spell of the quiet morning was broken. Davy finally had to say it. "I thought that guy, that Red Meredith, was going to kill you."

Neither Jack nor Doc answered.

"Well, I did," he repeated. "I mean, he was crazy mad or something."

"He was," Jack said, keeping his eyes straight ahead.

"But I mean, weren't you . . . weren't you . . ."

"Wasn't he what?" Doc asked.

"And then, how did you see that Korpec at the door?" Davy asked, switching to Doc.

"Because I looked behind me, Davy boy."

"That's why we sat there?"

Doc smiled.

Davy waited, then said to Jack what he couldn't keep inside. "You were so fast. I couldn't believe it. So *fast.*"

Jack said nothing.

"And then, when you ran out in the open with that Korpec guy shooting at you. I thought he hit you when you fell. That's why I came out there—I thought he hit you. I mean, you rolled over and over and at first I thought that one of his shots got you, I don't know, maybe in the leg or something, and you were there just a sitting duck. I wanted to do something, only he shot at me too. Weren't you scared or something?"

"I wasn't thinking about that," Jack said.

"Then, after that, I didn't know what was going on. I heard some more shots, and when I looked out all I saw was that you two were running to the backside someplace. I couldn't see what was going on. I mean, how did you track him down? He could've been anywhere. How did you know where he was?"

"Brains," Doc said, and laughed, drawing a smile from Jack.

"No, I really want to know," Davy said, the hunger for details rising clear in his earnestness.

"He doesn't believe it was brains," Doc said, "so what can I say. Maybe he doesn't believe in brains at all. Maybe he doesn't think either one of us has any brains. Is that it, Davy boy?"

"No, really."

"It doesn't matter," Jack said, but his tone left the key in for Davy to turn some more, because Jack once had the same passion to ask the same questions.

They rode in silence some more until Davy pressed on. "But he could've been anywhere," he said. "I mean, how did you find him? Nobody could see anything back there. Nobody knew what was going on. Everybody was too scared. I mean, I heard the shots, but I couldn't tell what they meant."

"I was a dead man," Doc said, and the way he said it was for Jack, not Davy.

But the words stopped Davy. He looked to Doc for more, and got nothing except a nod toward Jack. Davy held back as if to let the thought sink in, only he couldn't keep it there, the way Jack would have liked it. Finally, he said to Jack, "You saved him?"

That wasn't the way Jack would have put it. "Remember that Doc checked behind himself in the Road's End?" he asked Davy.

Davy nodded.

When Jack said nothing else, the young man's eyes showed that he understood. And still it wasn't enough. "But was that Korpec someplace in the back there?"

"He was there, all right," Doc said, and stopped.

"But where?"

"Jack found him."

Davy turned to Jack and waited. Nothing. "Where was he? How come you won't tell me?"

"We're telling you," Doc said.

"Not really."

"We had to kill a man," Jack said, his tone deliberate and serious. "Two men. It's not something to talk about. It's not something to be proud of."

"But I am," Davy said. "Of you."

Jack glanced at Doc, who knew exactly what Jack was thinking about when young kids talked of pride that went with killing. "Don't be," Jack said to Davy. "It's a mistake." He wanted to say more and to say it stronger, but that wasn't in his nature. He wanted Davy to believe him, to know that he knew what was important. Men in new, raw country could be on their own—had to be on their own—and this was a reason they were there in the first place. That freedom cost

something, and the toll was sometimes men like Red Meredith and Ned Korpec.

"At least you're proud that you could do it," Davy said.
"You're proud of that, aren't you? I mean, aren't you proud
that you're alive?"

"We survived," Jack said, knowing that this stark, essential,
authentic truth was disappointing to Davy. When the boy
clammed up, Jack was aware of the boy's disappointment at
not hearing the puffed-up details that he had expected. Jack
didn't live his life for admiration, and having Davy wasn't
going to change that. This was the second time he told Davy
that that gunfight in Caliente was about survival—not winning, not pride, not strutting around afterward like some
other men did. That path was a dead end, and Jack hoped
Davy could learn the lesson the easy way.

By high noon the three of them cast their shadows straight
down under the intense windless sky. Their shirts were
streaked with sweat down the crevice of their backs. The
horses were in need of water, and so was Davy. He reached
again for his canteen, only this time Jack asked, "Do you
really need it?"

That said to Davy, Don't. Wait. He put the canteen back.

"Up ahead we'll find some," Jack said, "but in case we don't
or it's dried out, better keep what you have."

The terrain rolled longer and higher as the miles added
up. The heat shimmied the distance, wavering the edges of
cliffs and the bulges of dry earth far off in front of them.
Sometimes the colors changed and vibrated, especially the
thin lines of reds from the land and the blues from the sky
reflecting off each other. When the land flattened in the
distance, lakes of shimmering blue stretched to the sides
where the land curved up again. These tricks of heat turned
the sky upside down when sunlight passed through the hot
air.

An hour later, Jack led the way up a narrow cutaway of

clay and sand banks. Then, when Doc and Davy caught up with him three abreast again, an abandoned shack in a long, curved row of cottonwood trees appeared. "What's that?" Davy asked.

"Salvation," Doc said.

"Water," Jack said.

"Let's get there," Davy said, anticipating the other two to kick into a trot.

"Take it easy. It's not going anywhere."

They kept a steady pace until they reached the shack, sun-bleached and gray, its roof slumped out of joint, the front door lying on the porch planks. A small makeshift corral to the left was strung with barbed wire; the shade roof was still in good shape. A half dozen buckets lay scattered around the wood-enclosed spring well. The cottonwoods near the shack rustled its leaves a little, sign that the heat of the day was boiling up its afternoon wind.

The bright shade of the cottonwoods over the well cut off the downpour of the sun like a faucet. Davy took off his hat and with his kerchief wiped the inside band, then the back of his neck and face. Jack and Doc brushed away the top of the water and studied it. The spring was good and flowing some. They scooped up two buckets of water and let their horses smell it before setting the pails on the ground for the animals to drink.

Davy did the same. When Jack and Doc drank a little water at a time, he did too, just as he copied the two men when they sank their wrists into the water and soaked their kerchiefs to put around their necks.

"The blood runs close to the skin here," Jack said of his wrists in the water. "It's a good place to cool your insides off."

"How'd you know this was here?"

"We've been here before."

"But there's nothing around. It's all dry creek."

"On top."

"That's what these cottonwoods are drinking," Doc said. "Look for some cottonwoods and you might find some water breaking through. That's why someone built out here."

"What happened?"

Doc shrugged. "Who knows?"

Jack stood up. "Nobody knows. We've never found anybody here. It's always been like this."

They filled their canteens, sat under the trees, and ate dried beef and hardtack. Jack was the one who got the other two to their feet and back in the saddle.

Four hours later, the accumulated heat of the day pressed hard on them as they followed a wide, dry canyon for a mile. When they emerged onto high ground, the dry wind picked up speed, hit them on the diagonal, forcing them to shift their heads away from it. The dryness sapped the moisture out of them, drained their strength. When Jack saw Davy's eyes glaze over and his lips swell and crack, he stopped and got him to drink slow and easy.

Before sundown they rode into Big Butte, about the same size as Caliente but with more closed-down stores and abandoned houses. The town was more compact too and set against a lone hard-rock mountain jutting up northeast of the town. Prospectors had found good veins of silver in it early on, and that brought more people. A few prospectors remained, but most of them left for California when the easy digging was done. Now the town was just another stopover on the way to someplace better, and where Sam Bates passed through.

CHAPTER 8

WHEN Jack, Doc, and Davy stepped through the batwing doors of The Shiny Bar, the saloon quieted in the usual way. Strangers got assessed in small towns wherever they went by whomever was there. But it didn't take long for the three tablefuls to go back to work, especially the four men in a boiled-up poker game. Two cowhands hunched over plates of beef and biscuits at a back table, a loner stared at his glass and bottle, a man and his woman ate and drank without a word or look at each other.

The Shiny Bar was a beans-and-whiskey saloon. The red-headed bartender wore a shaggy orange mustache and a smudged white apron around his front. He kept wiping his hands on it after delivering the food to the tables. "What can I do you for, men?" he asked as Jack led the way to the bar. Then, with a broad-cheek smile, he added, "Steak and beans, or beans and steak?"

Doc laughed. "Now, that's more like it—a real menu."

"I thought you'd like it. I'm BT, bartender and cook. Personally, I'd go for the beans and steak."

"You're on," Doc said, smiling, looking over the room with more caution than his mouth showed. "One beans and steak for me, BT."

"Best beans in the West. They've been mellowing in the pot for a week." He turned to Jack and Davy. "What'll it be?"

Jack leaned sideways against the bar so he could see the rest of the room. "Steak and beans," he said, smiling.

"That's good too," BT said, grinning and nodding to Davy. "You?"

"I'll have the same—steak and beans."

"Coming up," BT said, wiped his hands on his apron again, and walked to the kitchen door. "Won't take much except the frying," he called over his shoulder. "Take a table someplace."

"You think his beans are as good as he is?" Doc asked.

Jack smiled. "Are they ever?" He nodded to the corner table at the right front and led the way.

The poker players were slapping cards down like curses, laughing and chiding each other, taking turns scooping up the loot, having a good time.

BT stuck his head around the kitchen doorway and called out, "You men want some washing whiskey now or later?"

"Why?" Doc called back. "We supposed to eat those beans with our hands?"

BT bellowed out a laugh. "I like that. No, to wash down the dust in your throats. Or you want to wash down them beans?"

Jack glanced at Davy, and whether the kid saw it or not, the look was a reminder that he had to go slow with the kid. He was showing Davy that a big country took a big time to ease into it. "Sounds like we need it for the beans," he said.

"You got it," BT said and disappeared into the kitchen.

The loner scraped back his chair, stood up a little shaky, and left, pausing at the door to steady himself with a hand on the door post and adjust his eyes to the glaring sun. He looked at nobody.

One of the card players shouted, "I'm calling you, you big tub of lard, and when you see these you ain't gonna have nothing left in that dried-up old canteen between your legs."

Another laughed and slapped down his cards. "Read 'em and start blubbering to your mommie," he said, laughing and leaning his grinning face across the table. "Huh? You beat that straight flush ace high, you horny horned toad? Come on, let's see what you got?"

"I wouldn't show you dirt pies if you was starving to death."

The man bellowed a laugh. "Because you ain't got nothing. I knew it. Nothing."

"Yeah, you want to try again, you flapping buzzard?"

"I'm going to skin your bones white and then I'm going to stretch the rest of you out to dry. *You'll* be flapping in the wind when I get through."

"Deal 'em, deal 'em, 'cause I'm flattening you like that jack of spades, you bow-legged bushwhacker."

Davy smiled at the players. "They're having fun."

"Looks like it," Jack said.

"BT could bring a whole quarter side, as far as I'm concerned," Doc said. "I'm starving to death out here."

"Do you think any of them have heard of Sam?" Davy asked, still watching the players.

"Maybe," Jack said. "If Sam is drifting, he could pass through anywhere."

"Maybe I should ask them?"

"That's what we're riding for."

"Should I?" Davy asked, the question more of another permission from Jack than prompting for an answer. He waited with his eyes upward, searching for a release of guardian pressure that Davy both wanted and didn't want.

"Why don't you eat first?"

"They might leave."

Doc looked at the laughing, card-slapping poker players and said, "Doesn't look imminent to me."

Davy switched back and forth to Doc and Jack, weighing the prospects of showing them that he could make his own decision to stand up and deal with strangers just like they could. "But they might leave," he said, revealing that the prospects he saw weren't as convincing as he would like.

"There's plenty of time," Jack said. "Better eat first. I can smell it coming. We're all hungry."

Davy looked over at the players again. "They probably haven't heard of him anyway."

The players howled out another laugh and jeers at the next round of cards.

"I think I'll go ask them," Davy said, watching them over his right shoulder.

The look of self-doubt crept into Davy's eyes; the vacillation leaked through his insides to his face. He wore a wavering look of indecision with good reasons for yes and no. Being with Jack and Doc, two men who knew the country and what it demanded, weakened his resolve. Maybe it was the loudness of the poker players, together with a calm and confidence that the two men exuded just sitting there next to him. Whatever it was, he'd put himself in the middle of the creek, and Jack and Doc let him be the one to decide which way to go.

He slid his chair back, stood up, and walked to the card players, the high hard heels of his boots sounding loud on the wood-plank-floor.

The men made it easy for him. The one with the new blue kerchief around his neck over a faded, worn, ripped green shirt looked up and asked, "You want in, right? Go on, get yourself a chair."

The one to the right of him said, "Sure, come on."

"No, thanks," Davy said. "I was just wondering . . ."

"Come on, everybody wins here."

"It looks like it," Davy said. "No, I got some steak and beans coming."

"That's about all that *could* come around here." The others laughed, and then the green-shirted man slapped the deck on the table for the man in the brown-and-yellow shirt next to him to cut. He dealt the cards while the man opposite him tilted his chair back and blew out a slow, thick, acrid cloud of cigar smoke.

"No, I was wondering," Davy continued, trying to sound casual and composed, "I was just wondering if any of you ran across my brother coming through here."

"Yeah? Who's that?"

"Sam Bates."

The dealer halted in midmotion, glanced at Davy, and then continued. The other men stopped talking.

"He's my younger brother. We're looking for him. Have you seen him? I mean, did he come through here?"

"Sam Bates?" the brown-shirted man said, his voice hitting the last name hard, a heat simmering through.

"My brother," Davy repeated in reaction, almost a defense because he leaned back a little at the man's response.

"That son of a bitch."

"Come on, Al," the dealer said.

"That little son of a bitch *cheated* me," Al shouted, scraping his chair and standing up, charging around the table at Davy. "He cheated me right here, right goddamn here at this table." He grabbed Davy's shirt at the collar. "He owes me a double eagle. Where is he?"

Davy backed away, half pushing, half retreating. Both hands grabbed at the man's grip on him. "I don't know," he pleaded.

"He owes me."

"Sam doesn't cheat."

Al shook him. "You calling me a liar? You doing that? You calling me a liar?"

"No, we're looking for him, I told you that, we're looking for him." He glanced at Jack and Doc. But the two sat tight in their chairs, letting it happen.

Jack glanced at Doc, and the two of them decided to let it go. The card-playing men weren't armed, and it was time for the kid's baptism.

"Forget it, Al," the dealer said.

"Where is he?" Al shouted into Davy's face.

"I don't know."

"You're lying. Where is he?" he shouted, shaking and tightening his grip on Davy.

"I told you I don't know."

"You're lying like your brother. I hate that son-of-a-bitch

cheat. You're just like him. He owes me, the goddamn bastard."

The couple near the kitchen door stopped eating and stared. The three other men at the poker game twisted around to watch. Jack and Doc sat still in their chairs.

Then Davy did what he shouldn't have. His hands were useless against the man's strangle hold on his neck, so in desperation he reached up and clawed the man's eye-bulging face, digging his nails into his cheeks and forcing him to twist his head away in a yelp of pain.

With his left hand Al straight-armed Davy in front of him, hung him with his iron grip on his collar like a dangling rag specimen, jacked his right fist back to his ear, and smashed his knuckles into Davy's face.

The kid collapsed to the floor, his puppet legs and arms no help at all. Worse, he was still conscious. Blood dribbled from his nose.

Al bent down, grabbed Davy, and hoisted him to his feet. He cocked his fist again and flailed out. Only this time Davy held up his arms, ducking Al's fist and half-flailing in return, hitting Al on the same cheek that he gouged with his nails. That infuriated Al, infecting his whole body with anger. He lunged at Davy, pile-driving his left shoulder into Davy's gut and sending him breathless against the bar.

BT came rushing out the kitchen door. "What's the hell's going on?"

Al bear-hugged Davy's waist, twisted him, lifted him, and thudded him against the floor. The two of them rolled over, bumped and tumbled a chair on its side. When Davy was flat-back on the floor, Al propped himself on his knees, grabbed the kid's collar again to lift him off the floor, cocked his fist, and let loose. Davy turned fast and Al's fist glanced off his head above the ear. Then he shoved Al full force with both hands and a bellowing cry of exertion, sending him reeling and thudding to the floor.

Davy got to his feet, but Al was on his faster. Davy backed

away, finally free of the charging demon, except Al reached out with two long outstretched arms and with a snarl clutched Davy's shirt before he could get away. He pulled the kid back and stepped forward at the same time, his eyes blazing hot with mayhem in them. He cocked his fist again, holding Davy up and ready like a rag-headed mop he was going to sweep the floor with.

Jack scraped back his chair loud on purpose. Al heard it and saw him. "That ought to do it," Jack said, his voice iron steady and hard.

Al stopped his cocked fist. He looked over, his face frozen in the battle-tight ferocity that men get when they fight with rage in their guts.

Doc stood up.

"All right?" Jack asked. The cold, direct calm in his voice was such a contrast to the heaving, lunging breath and fight in Al that the two simple words carried an unmistakable threat.

Al stared across the room at the two men standing flat-footed and forward, hands by their sides, by their guns.

The other men at the poker table moved nothing except their eyes.

Davy just hung there, waiting, gasping, and cow-eyed.

Then BT did what he had to. "Al," he asked, "you want me to waste all this steak and beans?"

Nobody laughed, but the bartender made it easier for Al to release the kid and send him stumbling back to his table. The man that Sam Bates cheated stomped across the room hard and defiant, shoulders hunched, face scowling. He swung the doors banging against their hinges, and disappeared into the hot, dry sunlight.

Jack faced the card players. One by one they turned in slow motion to the center of the table and back to the game, less one. Jack sat back down, and then Doc.

Davy brushed off his pants, buttoned his shirt, tucked in its tails. He rubbed the base of his hand against his cheek and took off his kerchief, spitting on it and wiping the blood from his nose. He ran his fingers through his hair and looked at no one. BT came out fast with the food and set it all down. "Here you go, friends. We don't look for no trouble here. It's a good place, and I want to keep it that way." He turned to Davy. "You want to wash up?"

He shook his head.

"They're good men," BT said to Jack. "They like having a good time. It's just that, well, Al is hot-blooded as a blacksmith at times. He blows off the handle and ends up paying me for broken chairs, you know what I mean?"

Jack smiled, mainly to appease BT's good nature. "Did Davy's brother come through here?" he asked, nodding at Davy to see if the man named Al hadn't been making up campfire stories.

"Oh, yeah, he came through all right," BT said. Then he turned to Davy. "I know he's your brother. You look something like him, when I stop to think about it. But I'll tell you honestly, nobody here is much looking forward to seeing Sam again. Now, don't get me wrong. It's a free country; your brother can come and go as he pleases. But I got to say that Al's a pretty good judge of character. That's all *I'm* saying." He put a fatherly hand on Davy's shoulder. "I'm going to get you a cold, wet towel. Go ahead, son, it's chow time."

Davy didn't eat much. The more Jack and Doc satisfied their ravenous appetites, the more Davy picked at his beans and halfheartedly cut his steak. He didn't look up much. He didn't say much either, especially when Doc made a crack about how if Davy wasn't hungry anymore he could at least make good use of the steak by slapping it over his eye, which was going to look like a giant prune in a couple hours.

One of the card players called across the room, "Al's all right, you know. He just has to blow off steam. He won't be back."

Jack said, "Yeah, I know." He knew, too, that the man really meant Al wasn't one to come back with a gun, that the men stayed at the table to show Jack and Doc they weren't all going someplace for guns to back up Al. The message passed right over Davy.

"He's pretty steamed up about what Sam Bates did," the man said. "He's not the kind that forgets fast."

"It'll be all right," Jack replied.

"You know," the man said, "I heard about Sam." Then, to Davy, "He really your brother?"

Davy turned his battered face and only nodded.

"Well, you know, I heard he was up in Colorado."

"Why are you telling us this, friend?" Doc asked.

The man shrugged. "He's just a kid, Sam is, and he's going to get himself killed if he doesn't rein himself in some."

Five minutes later, when Jack led the way out, he stopped at the card table. He laid down a double eagle and asked them to give it to Al.

CHAPTER 9

THEY resupplied the next morning and rode north. Davy sat wordless in the saddle. The bruises on his face were little compared to his dejected spirits. He kept his bay mare two and three steps back and to the right of Jack and Doc. With Big Butte out of sight, Davy kept to himself, head bent, shoulders down. When Jack asked, "How's that eye?" he shrugged, looked away, and kept wordless another mile or so.

The mesas shrank in the distance as the three of them rode easy along the long, slanting desert floor. Yucca marked the flatness now and then. Mostly it was empty, horizontal country. The lay of the land in the short run dipped and rounded over dry creeks and low buttes, but the long haul was upward to what seemed an endless draw of the horizon. On and on the territory spread with giant vistas of human-less, treeless earth.

Davy was so immersed in his wounds that when at last he said to Jack, "Why did you do that?" Jack had no idea what he meant.

"Do what?"

"Leave that double eagle. That was Sam's debt."

"I thought it was better to close it all off."

"Sam should've paid him."

"Maybe, but he didn't seem to have a mind to."

Davy said nothing, because it was obvious that his brother wasn't about to pay up. Besides, who knew what really happened between Sam and Al?

After glancing at Jack, Doc looked over and said, "There's another reason, Davy boy. It means we don't have to waste time watching our backsides." Then he laughed. "At least not for Al."

"A double eagle?"

"Well, how much is your life worth? Or Jack's?"

"I can fight my own fights," Davy said, his mouth tight and thin.

"How old are you, Davy boy?" Doc asked.

"Seventeen. Why? What difference does it make?"

"It makes a difference when you ask why it makes a difference."

"I don't get you sometimes."

Doc smiled and went back to paying attention to his gray.

"We all need help sometimes," Jack said finally, looking at Davy straight-on, trying to convey to the kid that having friends when you needed them was all right. But he remembered that at Davy's age, pride and muscle were supreme, and backing down meant humiliation. Being protected by your elders was the worst fate imaginable.

He knew that Davy was running the scene over and over in his mind, how Jack and Doc stopped the fight when they stood up. Of course, it was humiliating, and maybe he shouldn't have let Davy get into the fracas in the first place. But what was done was done. They were traveling and leaving it behind in the dust. That was the point of this country—you could leave the bad past behind you and start over the next morning someplace new.

At sundown the three of them approached a wide-mouth canyon from the southeast. The failing light colored one side of the canyon talus a deep orange-red, leaving the other side a shimmering purple. They'd ridden to higher elevations, and the yucca and mesquite grew thicker, and piñon far off turned the land a little greener. What sagebrush grew around them was still not much higher than a hare's ears.

The canyon edges were cut by water runoff and funneled by flash floods to the canyon floor. Some sections of the red walls were polished clean, and from a distance they looked like razor-sharp cliffs that could slice a man in two if he fell on them. The floor of the canyon was gouged into a miniature canyon where the floodwaters from ancient times on had eaten away the sandstone and snaked out a hard-packed trail. Creosote bushes hung by desperate roots along the edges of this dry wash, and probably would be swept along in the next rain.

At the far end of this breach rose a giant mesa, far beyond the canyon itself but framed by the sides of the canyon. The mesa loomed like a mammoth anvil on which the sun ball rested ready for slapping and flattening. The base of the mesa was cluttered with huge fallen boulders fanning out like a billowy skirt. The mesa dominated the vista through the canyon, even though the colossal isolated rock stood guard four or five miles beyond the other end of the canyon. Two-thirds of the way to the top the smooth core of the mesa rose like a tooth of the earth the rest of the way to the sky.

The ruins were languishing on the side of the canyon floor, elevated enough above the floodwaters down the center and far enough from the flood-cut cliffs where the water spilled straight down. The farther the sun sank, the darker the ruins turned. Man-made walls of mud bricks stuck up from the blown sand that banked their base—nothing but walls and corners and exposed rooms in right-angled patterns.

"What're those?" Davy asked.

Jack cut his hand through the air for Davy to keep quiet.

Doc reined his horse in the same easy walk to the right, making a wide arc from the other two.

Davy looked to Jack for explanation, but Jack moved his forefinger once for Davy to keep with him. They rode the same slow pace along the caked hard red earth, weaving in and out scattered creosote and sage, heading straight for the ruins.

Meanwhile, Doc had ridden wide until he was at a direct

angle opposite the silent walls. Then he turned straight toward the ruins and sauntered in with a clear view of what was on the other side. Nothing.

Up close the ruins had the same kind of eerie silence about them. They looked half buried in the sand and protruded like worn bones from a grave, the edges of their exposed skeletons rounded off by the wear and tear of wind and rainwater. The ghostly part was that the walls were constructed with a startling precision of mud brick and chinks of canyon-cliff stone.

They dismounted and set up camp for the night. Davy followed whatever Jack and Doc did, fixing his bedroll in the protective fold of the ruin walls, because the slightest breeze without deflection sapped body warmth during the night.

When the sun disappeared, they replaced it with a campfire from gathered juniper. They ate dried beef, hardtack, dried peaches and apricots, and agreed to save the water for coffee in the morning.

"I should've used my gun," Davy said, staring into the fire, the small wavy flames casting an outside shadow of the kid against the ruin wall behind him.

The fight in The Shiny Bar had been gnawing at Davy all day. Jack let him be awhile before saying, "That wouldn't have been smart."

"I was dumb."

"That man didn't have a gun."

"So what?"

"You'd kill an unarmed man?"

"I should've drawn on him. That would've stopped it."

"Maybe."

"He sure stopped in his tracks when you stood up."

"But we didn't draw on him."

"Yeah, but he saw you carried guns. He knew you would use them, too."

"Maybe."

They let the soft hot crackle of the wood fill the black

silence around them. The night smelled of sweet unseen high air. A quarter moon lighted silhouettes beyond the campfire. The stars illuminated the rest of the sky.

Doc lay with his head propped against his saddle, fingers folded at his belt. "It's like these ruins, Davy boy," he said. "They're still here."

"What is this place, anyway?" Davy asked Jack. "A ghost town?"

"Ask the professor here," Jack said, nodding to Doc.

Doc laughed. "The professor says that these ruins are cosmic literature. They're what poets like Julia Older write about."

"They're what?"

"Cosmic literature."

Davy smiled and shook his head.

"You just have to know how to read them, that's all."

"Yeah, well, what do they say?" Davy asked.

"Nobody knows."

"That's for sure."

"Not yet, anyway. They aren't white-man walls. These walls have some exotic mysteries to them, but who knows what they are?"

"So they don't say anything."

"Sure they do. I can hear them right now. You hear them?"

Davy laughed. "Hell, no."

"They're saying it loud and clear. You hear those voices seeping out these walls?"

"Yeah, they're saying nothing."

"They're saying, 'Be smart, or be dead.' "

Davy sniffed and smiled and shook his head at the setup he'd fallen into. "They're just old walls."

"Right, Davy boy, dead old walls. But they weren't dead when people were living in them."

"Yeah."

Doc could get Davy to loosen up. Jack liked that. The wounds from the fight were fading already. Davy was laughing now, and Jack thought that the kid was healing fast, until they all went about their business of getting to sleep. That was when Davy broke the high desert silence, almost as if he were speaking back to the ruins. "I should've."

Everywhere they rode they left word that Davy Bates was looking for his brother Sam. Usually, they stayed overnight in a town to eat, resupply, buy some bacon and oats, wash up, and sleep on mattresses. In Silver Mountain, they talked with the proprietor of the general store, but he hadn't heard anything about Sam Bates. No one else had either. Silver Mountain was a dying town taken over by Ocotillo, a two-hour ride north. There no one had heard of Sam Bates either.

Most of the people were friendly. Some weren't. In Carter's Town, the blacksmith was suspicious. So was the owner of the general store. Even the women were hard-eyed and unsmiling. Nobody took to the strangers there. Doc said that it was probably an infection in town—nobody believed anything. The three of them rode out with no regrets.

The two days they spent in Santa Fe led to nothing. They stopped at the restaurant and bakery, the boot shop, the old Mission of San Miguel. They left word where they were staying and if anybody knew or saw Sam Bates to leave word the next day or so. Doc talked with an old Spaniard sitting in the plaza next to the Palace of the Governors; he'd seen no one called Sam Bates. Davy complained about a waste of time, but Jack pointed out that they were leaving a word trail behind and sooner or later Sam would cross it.

They rode out of Santa Fe, up and through the green mountain passes to the east, and on to the high sand-colored desert country north of the old town and ranges. Nobody at the stagecoach stations along the Santa Fe Trail had heard of Sam Bates. They watered their horses, waited out the scorching midday sun, ate some posole and tortillas, and rode on.

At Blue Hill in the bar a slicked-back cowhand in a red and blue shirt overheard Davy. He said his description sounded a little like a man he'd seen coming through town. He lifted his empty glass and stared into it. Davy bought him a shot of whiskey. Then the cowhand told him more about this stranger riding through Blue Hill and drinking at the bar a while back. He had been the spitting image of Davy. Davy asked whether the stranger had the same build as he did. The stranger said yes. Did he have hair like Davy's too? The stranger said yes. Older than Davy? No.

Then Jack asked him whether this stranger had the same color eyes as Davy. Yes, the cowhand said, but Jack pulled Davy away, telling the kid that this man was lying through his teeth—men didn't remember the color of eyes. "Just trying to help," the cowhand said, grinning. Jack pushed Davy along and over his shoulder said to the cowboy, "You got yourself a drink."

Davy realized that he was being played a sucker and moved to get back at the man, but Jack kept him going.

They rode on. At the base of Raton Pass they decided to hole up for a day and get themselves and their horses plenty of rest for the climb over the mountains. The pass was a steep cut in the high range where the thin air strained their lungs and slowed their horses. They stayed at a mining camp at the top of the pass, and talk there was circulating that the new Atcheson, Topeka and Santa Fe Railroad would cut out the aches and pains of freighting over Raton Pass in a couple years.

Two days later they were in Two Fingers, Colorado.

CHAPTER 10

TWO Fingers was a small clump of wood-slat buildings set in the vast grasslands slanting east from the Rockies. At a distance the colorless town looked like toys on the banks of a curving river. Up close it was dilapidated, full of broken windows and tilting doors. The store signs were weather-worn; the rain gullies in the one road through town were left unfilled. The town looked like a smithy at the end of a working day, with nothing but tomorrow just like it to look forward to.

The saloon didn't need a name; it was the only one in town. Inside was like the outside—raw and worn. Every chair was missing back slats. The tables were unvarnished and scarred with knife tallies from poker games. Dust balls and sand and smudges of mud filled the floor. The bar of sanded pine slabs was pieced together and mounted on a quick-sanded pine front. Half-empty bottles lined two shelves bracketed against the back wall. An old flintlock relic hung above the bottles, the only piece that was strictly decoration. The rest of the hangings were utilitarian—signs that said no food, no spitting, no fights, wooden hooks for winter gear, a coiled rope, an outdated calendar for 1875.

The bartender was tired and old. Gray puff balls of hair grew at his ears. He looked from under bushy eyebrows as if they were bandages, watching Jack, Doc, and Davy as they surveyed the hovel. Two young men and a woman sat drinking at a table near the far end of the bar. The woman was leaning against the dark-haired man, her forearm resting on his shoulder. He had his arm around the back of her chair.

The bartender nodded as Jack led the way to the bar.

"Strangers," he said in greeting. "What can I get you?" He didn't wait for an answer and brought out a whiskey bottle and three glasses.

"Thanks," Jack said, and filled the glasses.

"Where you coming from?"

"Through the pass."

"That chest thumper Raton, huh?"

Jack nodded.

"I've been there once or twice. Heading north?"

"Yeah, north."

"Looking for work? Cattle? Railroad?"

"No, looking for somebody," Jack said, and picked up the bottle and a glass and headed for a table.

They glanced across at the two men and woman. The man was kissing the woman like he was eating corn on the cob and rolling his hand in giant circles on her breast. When he stopped and looked over at them, he smiled to show his teeth through his bloodless lips, letting the womanless men know that he had something they weren't going to get. He took his hand off her breast but kept his other hand around her shoulder.

Davy stared wide-eyed, his mouth hung open. Then he turned away, as if he were intruding on something that he wasn't supposed to see. His eyes darted to Jack and Doc to see if they had noticed his naive embarrassment.

"Spectacle, Davy boy," Doc said. "It rules the world."

The bar bait looked at them, unsmiling, used to men. She brushed back her straight black hair; her blouse was open two buttons down. She was busy being bored.

The bartender put the bottle back on the shelf and leaned forward on the bar. Finally, he asked, "Who you looking for?"

Davy scraped back his chair before Jack answered and stood up. With glass in hand and an exaggerated show of confidence, he walked to the bartender as if he realized he needed to compensate for the forbidden spectacle he'd seen. "We're looking for Sam Bates," he said. "Ever heard of him?"

"No, sure haven't."

"Someone south said he'd be in Colorado."

"Big state, you know. We been a state two years, and what's it got us? Anyway, it's too big to know everything."

"We're leaving word everywhere. Sooner or later, he'll cross our paths. We've been through Sante Fe and Ocotillo and Carter's Town. No luck so far."

The dark-haired man with the woman chuckled.

Davy didn't notice that the man was chuckling at him. "I know it's big country, but if he does come through here, would you let him know we're looking for him? It's important."

"Sure," the bartender said, nodding, his lackluster eyes unconvincing. "Can't tell him if I don't know your name."

Davy laughed. "Oh, yeah. Davy Bates."

"He your pa?"

"No, actually, he's my brother. I got to talk to him about the farm."

"Some ranches around here, but no farms I know of."

"Back in New Hampshire. Back home."

The bartender nodded.

Then the young man stood up and sauntered to the bar, smiling and bobbing his head like he was holding back another chuckle. His friend and the woman watched from the table as he set his glass on the bar.

"Another one, Ed?" the bartender asked, and poured it without waiting for the answer.

"Actually," he said to Davy and chuckled, as did his friend, "you're looking in the wrong place."

"Yeah?" Davy asked, turning to the short young man leaning on the bar. "Why is that?"

Ed wore a cocky smirk and loose gun, the combination of a six-gun bully. He stood with both feet firm on the floor now and his hands at his side, but behind the even stance brewed an energy he was holding back. Maybe he didn't have enough to do, or he didn't like wasting his days the way he was. Whatever it was, he had a woman watching.

"*Actually,*" he said, the word out of place with the way his mouth curled up on one side, making it clear he was poking fun, "actually, nobody important comes through Two Fingers. Never."

Davy smiled, and said nothing.

"So you're wasting your time here. Better move on."

"No, I said it's important for me to find him, not that Sam is important."

"You calling me a liar?"

Davy stopped short, the same challenging words hitting him with the remembrance of the fight at the bar in Big Butte.

Ed's friend laughed loud enough to hear. Jack and Doc sat watching, letting Davy face what he had faced before.

"You calling me a liar?" Ed repeated, grinning from the side of his mouth. "Huh?"

Davy raised his head a fraction and squared his shoulders. "Listen, friend, I don't know what you heard, but I know what I said," Davy told him in as calm a voice as he could muster.

"You think I'm deaf or something?" Ed asked.

The bartender folded his arms and leaned back against the shelf of bottles. "Come on, Ed. Why don't you just take your drink and get back to Della."

Ed ignored him and kept his eyes glued on Davy. "Huh?" he grunted, provoking, playing with Davy like a coyote preying on a prairie dog.

Davy shook his head. "No, I'm looking for my brother. I just asked a friendly question. It's important that I find him."

His friend chuckled again. Della kept watching, expressionless. She looked neutral, but she wasn't.

Then Davy did something brash and sudden, as if the movement emerged from an undiscovered instinct. He took the glass in his hand, turned in slow motion, reached over, and slammed it down on the bar. It was a powerful noise, but the power didn't go into the sound. It went through Davy's core, into his eyes. He let loose of the glass and turned back to Ed.

He did something else that surprised even Jack and Doc. He straightened to his full lanky length, angled his eyes down at Ed, and asked, "You good with that gun?"

Ed's gaze revealed a shimmer of sudden doubt. The question came out of the blue like an ambush. "Yeah, I'm good, goddamn good."

And then, instinctively, Davy caught the momentum of his threatening question. Without pause, he asked, "You got good reflexes?"

"Yeah. Sure. The best."

"You fire off on everybody who comes in here?" Davy asked right away. As if he were opening a door to a simple trick of survival, he kept the questions coming. He was turning the tide around, *he* was doing the asking, and all it took was quick, fast questions.

"I live in this town, and you don't."

"What's the matter with people riding through?"

"Nothing, but I don't like . . ."

"What's the matter with asking a question in Two Fingers?"

"Nothing."

"Do you know what happened in Carter's Town when somebody like you came up to me?"

"I don't give a damn."

"You don't see any blood on me, do you? That tell you something? Because if it doesn't, it better."

"It doesn't tell me goddamn nothing," Ed said, sniffed, and bucked his head back, letting his friends at the table know that he still was master of the situation.

"Maybe it better, friend," Davy told him, his eyes unwavering. He stood taut-ready, his hands relaxed at his sides. He paused, and added, "Maybe it better."

The trip wire between then hung waiting for one or the other to touch. A silence pressed in on the two of them, an ominous force that crowded the saloon, like the press of cattle in a holding corral. Nobody said a word, nobody made the slightest movement, because the merest disturbance would crack-whip the balance.

Davy waited the seconds with the same deadly readiness as Ed. The difference was that Davy had slammed his glass on the bar.

Ed lost his smirk, but when he put it back on his face he signaled his move. He smiled and sniffed again, and in the same motion that was all part of the retreat, he looked away from Davy, breaking the hold and releasing the tension wire. He alluded to Jack and Doc, saying, "Yeah, with them two over there covering your ass."

Davy said nothing.

Ed stepped backward, slowly. "Not with women around," he said, shaking his head, and stepped back again.

Then Davy stepped back.

Ed turned sideways and eased back to Della.

Once out of town, Davy let loose of the internal flood of triumph that filled him. In the bar he was controlled and tense, even after sitting back down with Jack and Doc. But riding into the open country unlocked the floodgates to exultation and to celebrate the regaining of his manhood. He couldn't hold it back any longer. "Did you see that?" he asked Jack, smiling.

"I did."

"He back down. I called his bluff and he backed down."

"He did."

Davy turned to Doc. "Right?"

Doc turned and smiled. "Very impressive," he said, but the enthusiasm didn't match the words.

"I knew he wouldn't draw. He was just a wiseass kid. He didn't know anything."

"What if he drew?" Jack asked. "Then what?"

"I knew he wouldn't. I called his bluff. He was betting I wouldn't, wasn't he?"

"Maybe."

Davy shut up a few paces, but he was smiling broad and full. "Probably nobody stood up to him before," he said. "I took him off guard. He thought he was going to back me down, only he didn't. That's what makes me feel good about it. He had to change *his* mind."

"Why do you think he did?" Jack asked, swaying easy with the roan, looking over now and then at Davy, not reacting much to Davy's exuberance.

"Because I called him, that's why. He tried to bull over me, but I wouldn't let him, and he saw it. That's why."

"Do you think he thought he was outnumbered?"

"That's what he said," Davy countered, "but that wasn't the truth. He was shaking in his boots. I just stood up to him. It was easy. All of a sudden, I knew what I was doing. There was some point, I don't know when, but some point when I knew he'd back off. And he did, didn't he?"

Jack nodded. "What if he hadn't been outnumbered?"

"He'd have done the same thing. I mean, I was there. I could see the fear in his eyes."

Doc leaned over to catch Davy's attention. "What if he wasn't outnumbered and the woman was still there?"

"So what?"

"So plenty, Davy boy. What do you think got him to his feet in the first place?"

"How do I know?"

"The woman got him to his feet, that's what you should know. The spectacle of the world is lured by a sweet finger and a pushing hand, and don't forget it."

Davy looked to Jack for explanation and got only a smile. "Well," Davy said, "she didn't do anything."

"Ed was showing off," Doc said.

"I know that," Davy shot back. "He didn't do too good, though, did he?" He laughed.

"When a man has a gun," Doc said, his tone turning serious and unmistakably clear, "and his woman's there watching him, he's going to use it if he's got *less* than an even draw. If you ever see that combination again, take my advice and steer clear. Don't mess with a man and his woman."

Davy nodded like an obedient student, but his smile showed he didn't believe it. He looked at Jack for assurance.

"Doc is right," Jack said.

For the next week, whenever the three of them stopped to rest and drink, Davy walked to the side and practiced drawing and firing. At first he was drawing as fast as any young kid—slowly. As he practiced and concentrated, the crucial split-second differences showed more and more. He drew faster. And faster.

Jack and Doc said nothing of it aloud. They sat under a scrub oak and watched. His stance took on a studied determination, his body quick and sure. He honed down the wasted movements and reduced the distance between hand and gun, and gun and holster. Time after time, Davy drew and readied himself again.

"He's your sister's son, right?" Doc asked, angling his head as he always did when preparing the way for the real words to say.

"Right," Jack said, smiling, knowing something was coming.

"I like the kid."

"But what?"

"He can be a pain in the ass, that's what. What'd we get ourselves into? We've been riding around on a wild-goose chase, and he keeps getting himself into trouble for one dumb reason after another."

"He's just a kid."

"I know he's just a kid, but he's going to get us into trouble."

Jack nodded toward Davy working on his draw across the way. "You got to admire something in him."

"Right, he's improving himself. What worries me is that he's dying to *prove* himself, and I don't want to see him die trying."

"I don't either."

"But you got to admit, he's a bit of a pain in the ass."

Jack smiled and shrugged yes.

"Anyway," Doc said, watching Davy draw again, "being on the trail keeps Korpec out of Caliente."

Jack nodded at what really lay behind riding with Davy.

CHAPTER 11

THE town of Halfway served as a supply town for prospectors and drifters but also for cattle ranchers and cowhands, a sort of regional center, stockade, and trading settlement for the lone one-saloon towns within a day's ride. The town sported a weekly newspaper—the *Halfway Gazette*—with advertisements and town gossip, but the most-read columns were messages to men and women who passed through or rode into town now and then to stock up.

Jack, Doc, and Davy reined their horses to the left while a buckboard rattled by on the right. Small kids played jacks on the steps of the general store and were running up and down the boardwalk while they waited for their mothers buying what was needed inside. Halfway was a two-street town, plus some formless stretches of roadway on the outskirts where cabins and buildings were erected when the need arose. The other general store was at the opposite end of town. Scattered in between were three clothes and boot shops, a full-fledged bank, four saloons, two hotels (with cooks), and four other eateries. The town was busy. People were milling around and seeing what was doing. Two women in calico, with bundles in their arms, crossed the street on the diagonal toward the yard goods.

The Gazette office was next to the sheriff's. The woodfront bulletin board next to the door was plastered with messages, Wanted posters, and town notices. The front page of the current issue of the newspaper was tacked on. Above it read: "Buy the Halfway Gazette—A Sure Bet!"

Davy studied the wall from the saddle. "Hey, wait!" he

half shouted, and pulled reins. He leaned forward over the hitching rail and stared at the Wanted poster.

Jack and Doc watched him swing a leg over his bay mare and step onto the boardwalk, his neck stretched forward like a loose doggie. "What's he doing?"

Davy froze in front of the bulletin board. Then he reached up and ripped off the poster next to the front page. "Look at this!" He reeled around, marched back to his horse, and held up the half-crumpled poster in front of him.

> *WANTED*
> *Sam Bates*
> *for Murder*

Disbelief flooded the kid's face. All Davy could do was stare dumbfounded at Jack and Doc. All the innuendoes and doubts he'd met on the trail about his brother struck him like a punch in the gut. Jack knew that back home Davy always had known he was the flip side of his brother in Jessica's eyes, but here in black and white, the truth of their natures stared him in the face on the poster. It was in Davy's eyes: he felt they were both guilty. If his brother Sam was wanted for murder, so was he. What was to stop him from doing what Sam did?

Jack saw Davy's reaction and knew it was impossible to dismiss the fear that engulfed the kid. He knew that Davy hadn't yet learned that life in this country had to be taken as it came, not as it should be. Jack's calm resignation wasn't any less important than Davy's fear and bewilderment, but he knew Davy would take offense. So he dismounted and hitched the reins, as Doc did. "Maybe they mistook Sam for someone else," he said.

Davy crushed the poster with both hands and threw it into a trough. "I can't believe it," he said. "What'd Sam do?"

"Come on, let's get something to eat, then we'll find the sheriff and get some questions answered."

Davy turned around in frustration. "He's going to get himself hanged, isn't he?"

"He can take care of himself."

Davy turned around again, this time to see what the first time had caught his eye but didn't register. Another Wanted poster for Sam Bates was tacked to the front of the sheriff's office. He ran up the steps and ripped off the sheet just as the sheriff opened the door in slow motion and stepped onto the boardwalk like a cougar onto a cliff.

Davy froze in his tracks, eyes wide, his whole body caught in a confession of small theft and transgression.

The sheriff studied the kid a moment, nailing him to the nearest wall like a bothersome horsefly. Only his piercing needle eyes were needed to do it. Before he looked to Jack, he told the kid, "I hope you got a good reason to do what you did. You're tampering with the law, kid, and public property."

Davy opened his hand on the crumpled poster. "I was just . . ."

"Zeke, you old dictator," Jack said, walked up the steps, and stretched out his hand.

"Jack Tyson. I haven't seen you in a gopher's age." The sheriff and Jack shook hands. "And Doc, how are you?"

"Zeke, I haven't seen you since you got your nose smashed in Ocotillo a century ago."

Zeke smiled. "Yeah, well, I went straight—I got the star to prove it." He polished the badge with the tail of his kerchief.

"I thought we'd check out Halfway," Jack said. "Maybe get us a bite and rest up." He looked down the street. "The town's grown. You'll be hiring yourself ten deputies before long."

"Hell," Doc said, "Zeke doesn't need any Cerberus to guard against this Hades. When Halfway's ten times as big, then maybe he'll need an extra one of himself."

Zeke laughed. "Still talking teacher riddles, huh?"

"And that'll be some old decrepit codger who'll do nothing but reload his cartridge belt."

"If the town keeps growing and troublemakers like you come around here tearing up posters off the wall, you'll need more than book learning to get you out of jail." He winked at Davy.

"You still drinking pine sap?" Jack asked.

"I still got the bottle. Nobody else'll drink it except you two." Zeke turned to Davy.

"My sister's son," Jack said. "Davy Bates."

Zeke turned back to Jack, the reason for what Davy did to the poster now clear in his mind.

The way Zeke shook hands with the kid made it plain that if Jack and Doc hadn't been with Davy his reaction would have been different. The sheriff pumped Davy's hand twice and that was it. Never once did he shift his weight to one foot or the other. His body was compact and hard, his face sun-worn and unwavering in its line of sight. He had a strength in his dark eyes even when the banter and introductions were finished and done with. The thick dark eyebrows that went with his eyes added to the stern command of his face. It was what made him the sheriff, the difference between being a drifter and staying put in Halfway with the authority to interpret the town to his liking.

"Forget the poster, kid," Zeke said. "I've got fifty more ready to post all over Colorado. So you're his kinfolk."

Davy nodded, wary that the kinship spelled trouble, as it had in the past back in New Hampshire.

"I got a brother," Zeke said without going on. The way he said it left the message that his own brother, like Davy's, might be better left undiscussed.

Davy got the benefit of the doubt from Zeke because he was with Jack. It was a sign that he could be separated from Sam by a stranger, and a lawman besides.

"Come on," Zeke said and led the way into his office.

They pulled up chairs while Zeke retrieved a whiskey

bottle from a cabinet next to the gun rack. He lined up glasses on the table, poured one after the other, and passed them to his guests. Then he raised his glass and toasted, "To dirt and damnation."

Doc breathed out the first effects of the whiskey and held up the glass for examination. "Yeah, it's aged about as long as Henry David Thoreau went to jail."

"I thought you'd like it," Zeke said, and looked to Jack, waiting.

Jack took the hint. "We've been trying to track down Sam ourselves. My sister heard some news about him and sent Davy to find him and take him east." He nodded at another poster of Sam on top of the stack piled on Zeke's desk. "But we hadn't heard of this, did we, Davy?"

Davy frowned. "I know Sam wouldn't kill anyone. He's not a murderer. He's my brother."

"Nobody's a murderer until he kills somebody," Zeke said.

"It's got to be a mistake," Davy argued.

The sheriff shook his head, his eyes riveted on Davy.

"An accident or something."

"No mistake. No accident. It happened right here in Halfway, at the Waterhole Saloon down the alley. Too many people witnessed the killing."

"What happened?" Jack asked, seeing Davy was speechless.

"A card game, the way I hear it, and that's from everybody who saw it. Sam was winning and then he bet double or nothing, figuring he was on a hot streak and couldn't lose. Well, he got bucked off and went howling mad. He accused the man of cheating because he said it was impossible for him to lose riding a streak like that. He grabbed the stakes. The other man grabbed back. Sam pulled his gun and shot him in cold blood. He hightailed it out of town with two other hombres. Disappeared. I was at Deep Creek and didn't hear about it until two days later."

"The other guy pulled a gun," Davy said.

"Wrong. He wasn't armed."

Davy stared at Zeke. "Then the guy *was* cheating."

"What if he was?" Zeke asked. "You don't kill a man for cheating."

Davy looked away and drank more of the burning corn whiskey.

"He'd been in Halfway before and always made trouble," Zeke told Jack and Doc. "The killing's fresh in people's minds, and they won't rest until he's brought in."

"When did it happen?" Jack asked.

"About ten days ago."

Finally, Jack voiced what seemed to be on all their minds. "Nobody's going to like seeing another Bates face around town either."

"I have to confess to that one," Zeke said. "I agree with you."

"Well, I didn't do anything," Davy cut in.

"He knows that," Doc said. "That's why you're sitting here instead of back in the calaboose."

"You got a posse out for him?"

"Not yet," Zeke said. "Got some posters. We sent some by stage, and word spreads. But there's not much we can do, unless he's fool enough to come back to town. My jurisdiction's here. Besides, you know this town. Half of them are drifters, and the other half only use us as a watering hole."

"Which way was he headed?" Jack asked.

"East, they say. But who knows? I'll tell you one thing, though. A U.S. marshal came through here last week and said he'd heard Sam Bates had stirred up some trouble. He said he'd heard that Sam and two others were riding south along the Colorado–Kansas border. He came through Halfway when he saw one of the Wanted posters. From what the marshal said, I figured he was interested in Sam but had other priorities, a bank killing and a Fargo wagon holdup. I tried to convince him to go after Sam. It was Rab Wood. Know him?"

"Hell, yes," Doc said. "He'd haul in John Routt if he forgot to put a stamp on the envelope, just because he *was* the governor."

Zeke laughed. "Yeah, that's him all right."

"We ran across him in Caliente," Jack said, smiling. "He was riding after some Mexicans who stole cavalry horses."

"Well, he still reads the Bible on Sunday and shoots to kill the rest of the week."

"At least he can read," Doc said.

Zeke leaned to Jack. "I'll tell you this," he said, serious with his craggy sunburnt solemnity, his eyes back to the natural intentness. He stopped short, waiting for Jack to give the go-ahead.

Jack nodded slightly.

"Rab said Max Korpec had attracted some new men," Zeke went on. "He said Korpec had marked you for dead because you killed Ned."

"You heard about it all the way out here?"

Zeke nodded. "We should have a poster up for you, Jack."

"It was Ned's fault," Davy said fast. "He started it." His abrupt, defensive tone was out of sync with the conversation.

"Clam up, Davy," Doc told him, annoyed that the kid always spouted off the obvious and still couldn't tell who his friends were.

"Well, we can't keep leaving a trail of words," Davy said. "Not with Max looking for us."

"The only word I wouldn't leave around here," Zeke said to Davy, "is Bates."

That night, at a corner eating table, Davy kept talking about the trap the three of them were setting up for themselves. Sure, he wanted to find Sam, now more than ever. But if they kept leaving word where he could find them, Max

Korpec would get that word too. Korpec and his gang could just as easily zero in on them as Sam could. Only, Korpec was out to kill Jack, and Davy didn't want to be the reason that Jack got killed.

They better stop leaving word and just forget about it, Davy said. Especially now that Sam had a Wanted poster out on him. Besides, it was setting up Sam too. People who knew about Sam would just turn him in for the reward and forget about telling the three of them. Nobody could win. Besides, they weren't making any progress. It was turning into a long, useless, wild-goose chase.

Anyway, he continued, something went wrong with Sam. He wasn't a born killer; he wouldn't shoot somebody down in cold blood just over a card game. And even if it was true, where did that leave him? Brothers were alike, they had the same guts. And now he coudn't even mention his own name in town or he could be lynched because people *would* think that brothers were the same. If Sam Bates could kill in cold blood, why couldn't Davy Bates?

Jack and Doc listened. When Davy was talked out, Jack said to forget about Max Korpec. That was his problem. He told Davy that asking around about Sam was right, the only thing they could do that made sense and cut down on the time looking for Sam. Now that they had some information about Sam, good or bad, they had a decent chance of finding him. It was better that they find him instead of Rab Wood, wasn't it?

Davy nodded.

Doc slapped Davy on the back for encouragement and got a smile out of the kid.

The next day, they moved on to Red Top, Wyman, Blicker's Camp, and Scarecrow. It was in Scarecrow where they got Sam's message.

CHAPTER 12

JACK had ridden through Scarecrow two years before, and it looked the same, if not worse. Sometimes an outpost took on the look of its name, and Scarecrow was one of them. The buildings were a mangy group, half of them abandoned, a sign that this was part of the unlucky string of settlements that missed the ticket to the future. Maybe the name itself held its own fate, and what the people did—or didn't do— fate did anyway. Whatever the reason, Scarecrow looked older than it was. The core of the town was the hotel and saloon where a drifter could get a room, a meal, and a drink in one place before moving on. The buildings on either side of the hotel were abandoned. One was a hardward store, the other for saddles, boots, cartridge belts, chaps, holsters, jackets. That was the pattern. A restaurant still operating but two or three empty stores on either side—the empty store fronts on down the line. Behind the main street, brush had overgrown the paths to the outbuildings and shacks, leaving a scraggly first impression on the ride in. That was what Jack, Doc, and Davy saw.

The curious side of it was that whoever settled Scarecrow had a good eye for the country. The town was set high on a long sloping plain with foothills and a scattering of aspen. Young canyons led from the foothills.

Davy got the message from the Mexican woman behind the desk at the hotel when she asked him his name. She said that she was waiting for someone with his name. *"Un hombre* was asking for you," she said. "Here. He left you *una palabre."*

He took the sheet of paper out of the envelope and read it:

*Meet me tomorrow at Devil's Breath before sundown.
Alone.*

Sam

Davy held up the letter for Jack and Doc to see.

"*Gracias,*" Jack said to the woman.

"Oh, yeah, *gracias,*" Davy repeated. Then he burst into a grin. "Hey! He's here. We found him!"

Jack motioned Davy to the table. They sat down, and Davy slapped the letter on the table for all to see. Jack and Doc read it carefully. "Is that Sam's writing?" Jack asked, looking up at Davy.

"Sure. What do you mean?"

"Look at it again."

Davy twirled the letter around with his fingers and leaned over it. As an afterthought, he glanced up. "Why?"

"Because we don't want to ride into a trap."

Doc added, "Fools rush in where angels fear to tread, right? Well, fools rush in and often end up dead."

The revelation hit. "You mean Korpec?" Davy asked.

Doc let the thought simmer.

Davy leaned back to the letter and studied it again.

"It's called handwriting analysis, Davy boy," Doc said. "The name tells all. Is that the way Sam signs his name?"

Davy studied it. "Yeah," he said, his tone now grave and confirming. "That's it. That's the way he writes."

Jack glanced at Doc, and Davy caught it.

"That's the way he writes," Davy repeated with conviction as though they had no right to challenge something he knew was true. "I know my own brother's hand. We went to school together, you know."

"Good," Jack said, smiling. "It's better to be sure, that's all. We have to know what's in store for us."

"And who's tending the store," Doc added, slapping Davy on the back. "Cheer up. It looks like we found him."

Davy read the letter again. "But I don't know where

Devil's Breath is. I mean, I don't know anything about this town. It could be anywhere."

Jack nodded to the woman. "She'll know."

"Well, why don't I go out there now? He's probably there right now."

"We're going with you," Jack said.

"But he said alone."

"Two others are with him."

"He's my brother."

"He's not the same brother you know."

"Sam's still my brother, whether he's the same or not. What, you think he's going to draw on me or something?"

"I don't want you to get into trouble you can't handle."

"I can handle anything with Sam. Besides, you've seen me in action."

Jack groaned and Doc guffawed. When Davy showed signs of anger, Doc added, "Jack here is your mother's brother. He's beginning to think he's your father, too."

"But what if Sam sees us coming?" Davy asked. "He'll ride off. He said to come alone. He'll think I'm tricking him or I'm after the reward."

"Don't worry," Jack said. "We'll square it with him."

That night, while they were putting away enchiladas, frijoles, and carne asade, a man wearing a low-slung gun walked in, ordered a whiskey, and sat alone at a far table. He drank it in three gulps, taking his time, and sizing them up.

Finally, he put the empty glass on the table and asked, "You Davy Bates?"

Davy looked over his shoulder. "Yeah. Who are you?"

"You got the message?"

Taken by surprise, Davy turned around in his chair. "Yeah. You with Sam?"

Doc slathered pork fat on a tortilla, folded it in thirds, and took a bite, all the time keeping his eyes on the stranger.

Jack shifted in his chair to see the man better.

"He heard you were looking for him."

"We've been looking a long time. We covered a lot of territory, I'll tell you," Davy answered.

"Couldn't be helped," the man said.

"I just mean we didn't know how to find him. So we kept riding and leaving word where we were headed."

"Yeah," the man said, impatient, not caring one way or the other.

"So he's at Devil's Breath? Do you know where it is? I've got to see him."

"Who're they?"

"They're my friends. They want to come along."

The man said nothing, suspicion filling his eyes. The way his upper body tightened in a perceptible move backwards betrayed a sudden doubt.

"They're my friends," Davy repeated, as if the repetition was enough to allay the fear and make everything all right.

"Sam said alone, didn't he?"

"I know, but they've been helping me. I wouldn't have found Sam without them."

"That's not my problem. Sam said alone. I saw him write it. He said alone."

"What're you doing here, anyway?" Davy asked. "Why didn't Sam come?"

Doc reached for another tortilla. "He's just checking you out, Davy," he said, glancing up at the man and smiling. "Right?"

The man said nothing in return.

Jack looked over, his eyes making the point as well as his voice. "We're going with him."

The man waited. "Don't you get it? Alone means one, not three."

"Look," Davy said, "this is my uncle. He's Jack Tyson, and Sam knows him. He's my mother's brother. Just describe him to Sam, and he'll let him come."

The man rolled his glass back and forth between his thumb and forefinger. "I'll think about it."

"Where's Devil's Breath?"

The man nodded toward the señora. "She'll tell you, only he changed his mind. He wants you to meet him at the Junction. She knows about it. If he shows at all."

"Why wouldn't he?"

"I told you. He said alone."

Davy turned to Jack. "I'll be all right."

"You aren't going without us," Jack said before turning again to the man. "It's all of us or none. Take your pick."

"Let's put it this way," Doc said. "We're going along with Davy here. That makes it all even right from the start, doesn't it, friend? Three of you, three of us. One brother for you and one brother for us. Nice and neat. Nobody wants anything except what Davy here says he wants."

The man waited. "Who's he?" he asked Davy.

"He's Jack's partner, that's all."

The man stood up, threw down a coin for his drink, and walked to the door. "I'll tell him."

"What's your name, friend?" Doc asked.

The man debated with himself. "Pete," he said, and walked out.

Davy looked to Jack and Doc for some kind of interpretation. The three of them sat silent while the Mexican woman removed dishes and glasses. She had overheard everything, and sooner or later she was expected to give directions to the Junction.

"Smart," Jack said, glancing at Doc.

"Who, you mean Pete?" Davy asked, looking from one to the other, huddling toward them for reassurance.

"Sam," Doc said. "He's been waiting for us, checking us out, making sure Davy Bates is Davy Bates. You are, aren't you?"

After they finished eating, Davy stood up, shifted his holster against his hip, and walked out the back door of the hotel. He followed a barely visible path through the weeds and brush and passed a sagging abandoned shack with the ramada collapsed on the right side. He stood on top of a small incline, and there in the fading sunlight with the open country changing its shadows he planted his boots in the earth and time after time whipped his gun from his holster.

After five minutes of this, he held the gun at arm's length and emptied the chambers at a rock that skipped and chipped when he hit it.

He reloaded and put his gun back in his holster. Then he readied himself, feet apart, hand close to the handle, whipping his gun from the holster, the speed of youth at its height, and fired at the same stone, missing it by three inches. He returned the gun to his holster, drew, fired again, and hit close enough to move the stone.

Before he could draw again, a jackrabbit spooked from a creosote bush and hopped scared in a streak of zigzags, its long ears angled back, legs propelling the gray body with great leaps. Davy drew and fired at it, missing. He fired again and missed. On the third shot the animal tumbled, and Davy released the tension in his shoulders. He stood up straight, paused to pick up the rabbit by the ears, and returned his gun to his holster.

Jack and Doc watched from the back wall of the hotel.

The next morning, the señora said, *"Buenos, señior. Un momento, por favor."* She smiled at Davy and motioned him to come to the desk.

"Good morning, señora," he said, the force of the woman's formality and politeness drawing the same from him.

"Para usted." She handed him an envelope.

"Thank you. *Gracias.*"

"De nada."

He turned the envelope over and looked at Jack and Doc. "Who's this from?" he asked the woman.

"*El hombre*. He come late *en la noche* and leave it here. He say to give it to you *mañana*."

"The same man?"

"*Sí. El mismo*. The same," she said, her black eyes flashing. Davy ripped open the envelope and took out a scrap of paper. "It's from Sam. He wants to meet somewhere else."

"Figures," Jack said.

" 'Meet me at Lee's Mine at noon.' That's all he says."

"Did he sign it?"

Davy nodded. He studied the message this time; scrutinizing every word. "He doesn't say anything about you. I mean, he doesn't say if it's all right for you to come with me."

"It's all right," Doc said. "He's giving you leeway."

Davy looked to Jack and said, "But why doesn't he just say one way or the other? Maybe Pete didn't tell him about you."

"We're going, and that's settled," Jack said.

"But why change the place? That's the second—no, third—place he said. And he changed the time."

"He's a cautious lad, Davy boy," Doc said. "He has reason to be, from what we heard."

"I think he wants me to go alone."

"If he did, he'd say it plain."

"I don't know. And why'd he say noon instead of sundown?"

"He's just keeping us on our toes. It probably gives us just enough time to get there, and not before he does."

Jack turned to the woman watching the three of them. "*Señora, por favor*" he said, "do you know where Lee's Mine is?"

"*Sí*," she said, nodding and smiling. "My husband, he worked there."

"How far is it?"

"*Tres oras*." She held up three fingers. If they translated her Spanish correctly, she told them to ride east out of town until they crossed a dry creek. On the other side turn north and follow the ridgeline for thirty minutes, and then turn east again. When they came to a junction of two canyons, take the left one and follow it into the hills toward the mountains. Stay on high ground, she said. The canyon widens and disappears. That's where Lee's Mine comes into view. No one lived there now or worked the mine. Three buildings there.

"Cuidado," she said.

CHAPTER 13

JACK studied the layout as the three of them rode east toward the shacks. He expected Sam and his boys to be out of sight, hidden in the corners someplace, maybe even in the mine shaft itself. It depended on how smart Sam was, because they'd arrived before high noon and the sun angled behind Jack, putting the light into Sam's eyes. That is, if Sam was in the shacks.

Just as the *Señora* said, Lee's Mine appeared at the base of a sharp canyon wall, which in turn led to a steep bare-rock face. Three gray-weathered buildings stood in the open glare of the high sun. One leaned into the earth next to the entrance to the mine shaft where the man-size rectangle of the mountain tunnel was as black as coal. The other two buildings stood away from the mine and each other. Neither of them were much larger than one big room, relics of lonely, hard work, little monuments of hope and heartache against the stupendous might of the mountains that drove Lee, whoever he was, away to better prospects.

"What do you think?" Doc asked, drawing Jack's eyes to him and then motioning with his head to ask if they should split up and he should swing out and around as he always did when they approached a likely ambush. He didn't want them to end up a single target.

Jack shook his head. "He might get the wrong idea."

"He's not going to shoot us," Davy said. "Besides, maybe he's not even there."

"Maybe."

They rode at a steady uphill pace toward the shack on the left, giving free rein to the horses to walk the climb. The hooves knocked rocks out of the way, the horses snuffling and heaving as they kicked up the dry, slippery slag. Jack had his hand closer to his gun than usual. Doc's coat was folded away from his gun and tucked tight to keep it there. Davy, his caution unarmed, rode eagerly, and oblivious to possible danger lurking ahead. If the anticipation on his bright face was indication, all he saw was the hard-won reunion of his brother, the blood link that awaited him and his redemptive mission.

After the long wandering ride, finally Davy was going to meet his brother. To Jack, the search was youth remembered, and this was the reason for dragging an untested, unformed adolescent from one ramshackle town to another, keeping him out of trouble and alive. This was what the kid wanted, and now at last this was what he was getting. Maybe all the annoying bother was worth it.

Jack led the way to the shack on the right and stopped Doc and Davy with plenty of open space in front of it, space enough to include all three shacks and the mine-shaft together. They sat in their saddles, the sweat soaking their backs and arms, and said nothing, as if the torrid desolation of the place told them to wait without talking.

The heave of the horses' breath broke the hot silence, and the occasional restless kick of their hooves now and then broke the quiet.

Finally, Davy turned to Jack and half whispered, the silence somehow warning him, "Should I call him?"

Jack nodded.

Davy pushed himself up by his stirrups, as if he had to gain a few inches to make his voice audible. "Sam?" he called. His call sounded small and useless in the absorbing space. "Sam? You there?"

They waited for the return. Davy looked to Jack for explanation, but Jack kept his eyes ahead, looking from shack to shack and the red-rock boulders to the side.

"Sam?"

Nothing.

Then, from the back corner of the shack on the right, a man shorter than Davy stepped into the sun. He wore a dark green-and-tan-checked shirt, old and dirty. The rest of him was trail-worn too, his hair shaggy at the neck, his face rough with a three-day-old beard. He stood with a warning in his stance that had a lot of self-protection. He wore his gun snug and low, and the lean cheekbone structure of his face had the Bates look to it.

"Hey!" Davy called out in greeting, his hand stretching out automatically. "Sam!"

The rush of his family history forced a smile in Sam, and when Davy dismounted and rushed over to him, he stepped forward to meet his older brother.

Davy put his arm around Sam's shoulder and slapped him on the back. "Damn, it's good to see you," he said. "We've been all over the world looking for you. And this is one hell of a big world. We left word everywhere we went. You look different—like you've been here all your life. What about this shooting? I heard you got in a shooting. I saw a poster on you. What the hell is that all about?"

Sam's face filled with a sudden suspicion. "Why? Are they looking for me in town?"

"There's a poster on you," Davy said, but he couldn't keep on the subject. "How're you doing?"

"I'm doing all right. How's mother? What're you doing out here, anyway?"

"She's worried about you."

"There's nothing to worry about, unless you're bringing me problems. I said to come alone."

"I was really hoping you'd catch wind of us sooner," Davy said, ignoring the statement.

"Well, I did," Sam said, smiling against his will. He glanced at Jack and Doc, still mounted and watching them.

Jack nodded. "Sam," he said. "Good to see you."

"Jack. I heard you were here in Colorado. New Mexico,

though, mostly, huh? Guess I never got a chance to look you up."

"Guess not," Jack said, turning to meet the eyes of the two men who stepped into sight, figuring their horses were tied behind one of the outcrops of boulders.

Pete came from the back of the shack on the left. The other man stepped from the entrance to the mine, the rifle in his hand pointed down at his side.

"You know Pete already," Sam said. He pointed behind him. "And that's Tom."

"This is Doc," Jack said.

Sam nodded.

"So," Davy said, the jubilance still in his voice, "how are you? You look skinny. Your clothes are falling off."

"Colorado does it to you."

"Yeah, I bet. How long you been out here?"

"Here?"

Davy nodded, smiling, not really caring what the answer was because the question was filler talk that welled up from his excitement.

"We've been waiting for you."

Jack and Doc kept their watch on the two men at cross angles to them. They kept to their horses, high where they could see better. "Your mother's all right," Jack said, making clear that it was high time for Sam to focus on Jessica.

"Yeah? She is? That's good."

It was Davy's opening, as if Jack were nudging him. "She's worried about you." His face turned serious.

Sam stepped back a stride. "She doesn't have to."

"She can't help it."

"I'm doing what I want to do. She should worry about you. You're the one who's still wet behind the ears. What're you doing here, anyway? You don't belong out here."

"I came out to see you."

"You should be back at the farm, digging potatoes.

What'd she do, send you out here to drag me back? I'm of age, you know. I got my own life."

Davy stepped back the same as Sam, but the reaction was a mix of affront and surprise at the curt turn of Sam's tone and attitude. "No, she didn't send me out here to drag you back. She's worried about you. She heard you were getting into trouble, and she's right. You're in big trouble, aren't you?"

"She heard wrong. I'm not in any trouble. What do you mean, she's worried about me? Since when?'

Davy stared wordless at him.

"You're the one she's always worried about." Sam stepped to the side, all the time facing Davy. "You're older, so you're first. You were always her favorite back there: 'Give Davy this, give Davy that.' Well, I'm not back there anymore."

"That's not true at all."

Sam's eyes blazed with sudden anger, the threat to his truth. "The hell it isn't. You got first choice in everything. 'Where do you want to go, Davy?' 'Have some more pie, Davy.' 'Let Davy go first because he's your older brother.' So don't tell me about it. I *know*. I know you were always the one she worried about."

"No," Davy said, shaking his head. "That's not the way it was."

"The hell it wasn't."

"Then why did she want me to come out here? Because she's worried about *you*, that's why."

"It's the farm that needs me, not her."

"She wants you." Davy gestured to his brother. *"You."* His words turned soft, almost pleading. "She's afraid you're going bad."

The switch didn't take. Sam stared back with the same hard eyes and tension that grew and stayed in his neck and arms. "What does she know about anything? What does she care?"

Davy reached into his back pocket and pulled out the

crumpled Wanted poster. He unfolded it, snapped it straight, and held it up, one hand on top, the other on the bottom. "Did you see this?"

Sam stared at the sheet, his reaction masked with practiced indifference. "No. Why should I?"

"You didn't see this?"

Sam looked from Davy to the poster, back and forth. "Why the hell should I? I don't give a goddamn about that. If you believe that, you'll believe anything. It's a bunch of lies."

"You killed a man."

"I didn't kill nobody!"

"The whole town says so."

"What goddamn whole town?"

"Halfway. You killed a man over cards. That's why they got this poster out on you."

"I didn't kill any goddamn man over cards."

"They saw you, Sam. They saw you kill him."

Sam pointed at Pete and Tom standing like sentinels from their positions of defense. "Ask them. They were there. I didn't kill nobody. Sure, I play cards, that's what I do. I'm good at it, and I was winning. I won the goddamn game, only the son of a bitch wouldn't admit it. He couldn't bear losing that big pot. He grabbed it, and I grabbed it back. I won it fair and square. Then he drew on me."

"He wasn't carrying a gun," Davy said fast.

"The hell he wasn't."

"They all said he wasn't."

"Sure, they said he wasn't. They live there, they knew the bastard. It's their word against mine. They're bound to lie against me beause I don't live there, I just win their money."

"Then how come he's dead?"

"Because the goddamn whole place went crazy, that's why. I got the hell out of there. They weren't going to let a stranger get away with their money. Somebody else drew on me too. You think I'm going to stand there and get hit? Hell no. So I drew, and they started shooting. Everything went up in smoke, and there was a free-for-all. I don't know how he got shot, but I didn't do it. I just wanted to hightail it out of town. And that's what I did." He pointed to the poster. "That thing is a lie, and they know it."

Davy paused, crumpled the poster again, and threw it on the ground.

"They're lying, because I won and they couldn't take it."

"Then why don't you go back and tell them?"

Sam laughed. "You're really green, you know that? Really green. They'd hang me soon as I rode in. Hell, no, I'm not going to do that."

"Are you going to keep running forever?"

"Why'd you come here, anyway? To ask me stupid questions like that? If you stick on my trail, I really will be in trouble."

"I told you."

"Well, I'm out here where I belong, and I damn well can live my own life."

"You belong with the farm," Davy said, taking an opposite step. He and Sam were circling in the dust like penned bulls.

"You belong on the farm, Davy, not me."

Davy changed his tone. "Come on, Sam. Come on back and work with me. Let's work up the farm and make something big of it. We can do it together, a team. Mother can't work it herself without both of us."

"Go back yourself. I don't want any part of it. Out here, I'm free. Back there, I'm a workhourse plowing up nothing *for* nothing."

"It's our farm."

"It's all yours—is that what you want me to say? Go ahead, take the damn farm, it's yours."

"You're ruining your life."

"You're so dumb," Sam said, shaking his head, laughing,

sneering, his eyes once again blazing. "You don't know a goddamn thing. I told you, and I'm telling you once and for all—I don't want that goddamn farm. I hate it. So get the hell out of here."

Jack steadied his horse and kept his hand by his holster when Sam pulled his gun and raised it level at the shack. Davy leaned backward as if the few inches would save him if Sam turned the barrel on him. Doc edged his hand toward his holster; Pete and Tom alerted themselves to what was happening, what could happen.

Sam held his gun out arm's length, an unconscious signal that he was not in an attack on them or he wouldn't have wasted the vital second that a straight elbow and prolonged aim took. He pulled the trigger and blasted the front window of the shack. The glass clinked and shattered and collapsed; the horses jerked and bucked; the gunshot sound reverberated against the face of the mine.

Davy regained his equilibrium and stared at his brother.

"That's what the hell I think of the farm," Sam shouted. "So get the hell out of here and leave me be. This is my country, and I'll live in it to suit myself."

A cutting, alert silence swept over the men while Sam held his smoking gun.

Jack said, "Better put it away, Sam."

Sam looked to Jack, waited in the balance between threat and foolishness, and jammed his gun back into his holster.

The violence of the shot, and his utter contempt for the farm, marked a silence between the two brothers deeper than the life the farm had given them. They waited for each other to move.

"Don't you see what you're doing, Sam?" Davy said at last. "You're drifting around, gambling. Now you're wanted for murder. You're my brother. I don't want a brother turning into a no-good gambler and killer."

Sam pointed at Davy, his finger a barrel, his eyes refired

with rage. "You ain't no brother of mine. So get the hell out of here."

Davy turned on his heel and mounted his horse. He shouted back, "You'll end up dead."

"You goddamn stay out of my way," Sam shouted, "or I'll send *you* back in a casket."

CHAPTER 14

THEY followed Jack's suggestion to return to Scarecrow to rest up and decide what to do after the heat of the encounter had cooled off. Along the way, Davy fumed with black thoughts of what he was going to do. "I'll *drag* him back, that's what," he said. "I should've done it back there, right there when I had the chance."

"He's not interested," Jack said, his calm matching the other side of Davy's storm.

"I'd make him. He's my brother."

"You're *his* brother, too, and he didn't say much about keeping you here."

"He's an outlaw, Jack. I mean, he's on a Wanted poster and doesn't even care."

"I've got an idea," Doc said. "Why don't you rope him? Tie him up and drag him back that way. He'd get a rope around his chest instead of around his neck."

Davy turned to Doc. "It's not a joke, you know."

"Easy does it, Mr. Bates," Doc said.

They rode in silence until Davy said, "He's going to get himself hanged if I don't get him away from here."

"He might," Jack said. "But he's his own man now. This country makes you wise up fast. Davy, he's your brother, and that's the reason you came out here after him. Now you have to decide if your reason has changed."

Davy looked to Jack for more advice, but Jack kept quiet.

"Davy boy," Doc said, "he means that you have to figure out if you want to drag Sam back because he's headed to hell or because he's defying you, and you can't stand it."

"I can stand anything."

"Maybe you can. What about the other side of it? What if you fail? What will your mother think? What'll she say? What if you become known as the brother of Sam Bates, the killer on a Wanted poster?"

"That's not it."

"It isn't?" Doc asked. "He's your younger brother, and younger brothers are supposed to do what older brothers say."

"I don't care what he does."

"Sure you do," Jack said.

The ambush caught the three of them in a thunderous crossfire, the sound of the shots cracking and exploding their conversation into shouts.

"Get down!" Jack yelled.

They hugged their horses' necks and galloped to the only side of the red-rock canyon that was free of gunfire. Jack and Doc grabbed their rifles and jumped from their saddles. In panic, Davy ran low to the double cover of cracked boulders. Their horses strayed to the side, nervous from the shots.

Bullets zinged past them. Some of the lead hit the dust and chipped the soft rock around them, closing them in like an invisible net.

The barrage stopped as suddenly as it started.

Davy squeezed into the crevice, leaned back against the cold boulder. He was panting from the fear and complete shock of the ambush.

Jack and Doc faced the gunmen, their hats off so they could inch their heads and eyes up to study the lay of the land without exposing themselves.

The shallow canyon was strewn with cabin-size boulders. The east side rose high in the midsection where the hard-pack had resisted the erosion and left only shadowed cavities after huge chunks had fallen away. The three of them had spaced themselves in a row behind the quickest cover they could find. If they didn't move fast and right, they could be squeezed to death.

"Sam," Davy said. "It's Sam. He trailed us."

"Quiet," Jack ordered.

Three more shots splattered the boulders in front of them.

Jack and Doc ducked down. "You see them?"

Doc nodded.

They crouched lower. "We have to force them out," Jack said.

"Wait," Davy said, his disbelief raising his voice. "You're going after Sam?"

Jack kept his eyes and ears alert to the gunmen on the other side of the wall of boulders.

"Jack?"

"Stay put," Jack hissed.

Davy turned around and propped himself up. "I'll call him."

Jack quick-stepped in a crouch and grabbed Davy's shoulder, pressing him to the ground. "Did you hear me? Do as I say. Keep your mouth shut." The heat in Jack crushed Davy to submission.

"Jack Tyson!" the man called, the echo of the voice ricocheting from boulder to boulder. "You're a dead man, Jack Tyson. Hear me?"

Doc told Davy, "It's Max Korpec."

The name imploded on Davy's face, producing a bizarre combination of relief and realization that Max Korpec had picked up their trail and followed them to Sam.

"You hear me?" Korpec shouted. "A dead man. You killed Maggie, Tyson, and now I'm going to kill you."

"He's behind that big one on the left, with the three cracks," Doc whispered. "Cover me."

Davy moved closer. "What're you going to do?"

"There's some cover to the right. Not far."

"But three of them!" Davy said.

"Four," Doc corrected.

Jack nodded.

Davy looked from one to the other, amazed that they had spotted four when he was guessing three. He had made a critical mistake.

"We need you," Doc said fast. "Can you handle it?"

Doc was the one who joked and made fun of him. Now he was seriously asking Davy to play a role vital to their survival. Davy nodded

"We have to get out of this box," Jack said, directing his words at Davy but his eyes toward Korpec, "or they'll close in. I'm getting over there. Doc will move to the left. You're going to hold here. It's important. We need to break up their focus."

Davy nodded, excited by the prospect, sweat beading on his forehead.

"When you're firing," Jack said, his eyes demanding Davy's attention, "keep it low. Move your position if you have to."

Davy nodded, his eyes wide with the instructions.

"You understand me?"

"Yeah."

Korpec and his men fired another barrage, forcing them to press tighter for cover.

"Tyson?" Korpec shouted when the shots stopped. "You're a dead man. We've got you pinned. You hear me?"

Jack looked to Doc and said, "Let's keep them there."

They waited a second, reached up at the same moment, and leveled their Winchesters at Korpec and his men, firing in quick-lever action, forcing Korpec and his men to duck out of sight, pinging and shattering the rocks that hid them.

When they each had fired off four shots apiece, they slid back down where Davy pressed against the boulders, waiting.

Korpec fired back.

"They're going to move in," Jack said.

"Let's do it first," Doc said. "Two tens?"

Jack nodded and turned to Davy. "You listening?"

"Yeah," Davy said, nodding, his eyes unblinking. "Yeah, I'm listening."

"I'm going first. Doc and you are going to cover me. When I get there, he'll count ten."

"One, two," Doc said aloud to Davy, and cut the edge of his hand through the air in steady rhythm. "Like that."

"Then I'm going to count," Jack continued, "and at ten he's going to get over to the right there. That's when you get up and fire like hell. I'm going to cover him from over there. At *ten*. Both of us exactly at the same time. You got it?"

Davy nodded.

"Then we'll count again. At ten, we're both going to circle in on them closer. You'll draw their fire again, and we'll move in. Got it?"

Davy nodded. "Then what?"

"We'll see."

"Where do I go?"

Jack pointed to the ground. "You stay here. Don't move. I want you right here."

"Remember," Doc said, "there are four of them. So don't go to sleep, Davy boy."

Korpec's men fired another round.

Doc told Jack, "We got to move."

Jack nodded. Then to Davy he said, "They're killers. They're going to kill you if they can." He motioned to Doc. "Let's go."

Jack and Doc pressed against the outer edges of the huge boulders, crouched for a sprint, and looked over their shoulders a moment at each other. A second later, Jack sprang into the open.

Doc leaned into the deadly open gap and fired round after round. Davy reached up and fired his Colt.

Korpec and his men fired back at the boulder and then aimed at Jack. Too late.

Jack tumbled safe behind the eroded rocks at the base of the cliff.

Doc ducked, cut his hand through the air for Davy to see, counting aloud with crucial rhythm, matching Jack's unseen count.

At ten, Doc ran to the other side while Davy reached up again and fired, emptying his chambers too soon while Jack blasted his Winchester faster than Davy.

Davy slid back down and jammed more shells into the chamber, all the while counting in the same rhythm. At ten, he pointed his gun barrel over the boulder and fired again, this time into splinters of rock that were exploding around him.

Then silence, because they were all reloading, in a panic not to be caught empty.

Jack fired at Korpec, chipping the sandstone and forcing the men behind it.

Two of the men fired back at Jack, sending him to dive for cover.

Doc fired at them from the side. They turned fire on him, but Davy's shots from straight on were too much and they ducked out of sight. The triangle they had set up was working.

A fourth volley veered between Davy and Doc.

Meanwhile, Jack crawled the circumference of a noose to tighten around their rear guard and reverse their own strategy. But it was high risk. Doc and Davy were now on the other side of the gap, and he was cut off from them.

Korpec caught on. "Tyson!" he shouted. "We got you, you son of a bitch, and we're coming to get you."

Korpec reappeared long enough to say something low to his men, point his rifle for them to move in on Jack from two directions.

Jack saw the countermove. So did Doc, who fired off at two of the men maneuvering to get wide of Jack, pinning them back down before they got too far.

Davy moved to the other edge of his cover and fired at one of the men, sending him scamperng for cover.

The diverted seconds gave Jack the extra security he needed to run to higher ground. His boots dug into the loose earth. He slipped enough to make him a full-bodied target.

Doc fired at one of Korpec's men.

Davy fired at Korpec, half standing and eager for the kill. The shot forced him down.

Jack caught hold and finished the spring, diving for the protection of a fallen ledge.

A lull fell over the standoff. Here on their own, Korpec and his men had no restraint of a town or sheriff or marshal, free to consummate the revenge of Maggie. "You killed my sister," Korpec shouted, this time with ragged hate in his voice, the kind of uncontrolled dominance that vengeance could gain. "You're dead! You hear me, Tyson?"

Silence was the only answer.

"You hear me? You hear me, Tyson?"

Still nothing from Jack.

Korpec gave a muffled command to his men.

Jack gauged the height from his cover to a higher advantage. It could work, because he already was higher than Korpec and his men now. They'd be looking up enough so that their angle of vision would miss the flat of his back as he crawled.

He held his rifle outward, crouched down, and crawled as fast as he could behind the half-ledge, scraping his hands and chest against the sandstone, inching across the deadly open space. He heard a thud of boots below him, but no shots. The men were repositioning, closing in.

When he reached the other side, he crawled the extra foot, careful not to expose his position. If he figured right, he'd be where they wouldn't expect him.

He heard Korpec's voice, not understanding the words.

And he heard the heavy sound of leather boots on the ledges. Not one pair, but three.

Doc fired from the far side.

Korpec returned the shots.

Jack crouched to the edge of his cover and fired once at the three men closing in. Korpec wasn't with them. He sighted the rifle on the second man, slicing chips of canyon wall, forcing two of the men to dive behind boulders.

The third kept running toward Jack.

Korpec sent a barrage at Jack.

Doc forced Korpec down.

Jack swung his rifle out again, a second after the sound of Davy's Colt firing once, twice, three times. On Davy's fourth shot, the reckless, running fool of a man collapsed like an anvil to the earth, his arms flailing out, rifle clanking to the rock, his chest and face hitting blood and bone against the unforgiving rock and bouncing his heavy carcass once, dead before he hit the ground.

Jack fired from his new position at Korpec and the other two men. Doc from the rear.

The men cowered under the encircling attack, and with one of their own killed in sudden gore before their eyes, they slipped back through the shallow maze of boulder cover to their horses and rode off with Korpec, all of them kicking dust in a retreat, leaving Davy Bates standing triumphant and trembling with his first kill.

CHAPTER 15

THEY watched Korpec and his gang ride off, their dust dissolving into the distance, their shirt colors and riding shapes fading through the shimmering heat waves that undulated over the rolling terrain. They waited to see if the ambushers would reappear, but they didn't.

Davy looked toward the body; it was hidden behind an outcrop.

"Come on," Jack said, getting the kid's attention and moving toward the dead man.

"I'm shaking all over," the kid said, his voice cracking. "I can't."

"Sure you can."

"I'm shaking," he repeated, as if he couldn't believe something like this could dominate him this way, something he couldn't control. His eyes were questionng the twist of reality in him, his mouth hanging open in disbelief.

"It's normal," Doc said.

"I never did anything like this before."

"We know," Jack said. "Come on. You're shaking because it could have been you instead of him. It's all right. In fact, it's good."

Davy looked to Doc, who nodded at the truth of what Jack said.

"Come on."

Jack led the way down a short incline, over the other side, and then to the outcrop. He stood on the top. Doc stepped next to him, but Davy lagged behind, stopping before he reached the top.

"Come on," Jack said, his gesture stronger than his words.

"I don't think so," Davy said, shaking his head.

Jack waited, his eyes on the kid, drawing him the final few steps where he would see what he had done.

Davy stepped to the top and stared down at the body. It lay in a grotesque spread of limbs impossible in life, its arms angled like a gnarled stunted tree, one leg bent under the other as if the knee had a backward hinge. The man's face stared up at the searing sun and his killer Davy Bates. His open mouth released a thin trail of blackened blood already drying on the man's jaw.

"You had to do it," Jack said as the three of them looked down.

"He was too far away from me," Doc said.

"He would have killed me," Jack said.

Davy looked at Jack in a futile search for justification and absolution. Was what Jack said the truth or merely reassurance and justification of what he had done? Neither Jack nor Doc thanked Davy. That in itself was a lesson in taking advantage of the chancy opportunities of fate. Survival of each of them in the gunfight was based on working as a single mechanism of smart, careful, resourceful men, one relying on the other. Thanks was irrelevant.

"What'll we do with him?" Davy asked.

"Leave him."

"But shouldn't we bury him?"

Doc turned and said, "He would have tried to kill you next."

Davy said nothing. He stared down at the man.

"The vulture'll get him," Doc said.

"Let's go," Jack said as he walked away.

When they mounted up, Jack caught Davy's attention and raised his head toward the sky. Three huge black vultures swirled through the thermals in smooth, languid, overlapping circles, each swirl moving them closer. In the distance, black dots against the cloudless blue were growing larger and moving in. Davy studied the sight with amazement, his face showing the innocent astonishment at the speed of discovery that these predators displayed. How the vultures knew of the carcass in the middle of nowhere was surprising enough, but the speed with which they approached in such calculated smoothness was mysterious. A man's death in the open fed the brutality of the country. A quick rawness between man and his ultimate predator lay behind the sleek coming of the vultures. The sight had another message that tainted the shine of innocence.

They loped back to Scarecrow. The words among them were few and far between, mostly limited to comments about which way to go and recognizing landmarks.

Jack knew enough about gunfights to know that Davy was going over the scene time and again in his head, remembering the moves, the unpredictability, the risks that succeeded. He knew that the true threats were melting away by virtue of the successes, and how the triumphant feeling of survival enlarged the inevitability of the outcome.

The closer they got to Scarecrow, and the farther from the gunfight, the more Davy loosened up. After a while he said, "We outgunned them with three of us, didn't we?"

"It's what you do with what you got," Doc said, "or as they say in Latin, *Nemo dat quod non habit.*"

"You're really something," Davy said, smiling and shaking his head. "I don't know what you're doing out here."

"What we all are doing—searching."

They rode along the edge of a dry creek, the creases in the earth etched sharp by the wind and kept clean by the baking heat.

"It was a good thing I practiced," Davy said. "I mean, if I didn't know what I was doing, it could've been bad back there with Korpec, couldn't it?"

He rode in silence until he had to bring it up again. "If

I hadn't had some skill in my gun," he said, "things would've been different."

"Doc was there."

"Doc was way over on the other side."

"He had a rifle," Jack said, and this time turned to Davy. He didn't say that Davy forgot his rifle in the panic to run for cover, but the meaning was there. The clipped way he said it emphasized the implication of what that panic could have meant.

"All right, I didn't have my rifle, but I didn't need it, did I? It turned out that way. I didn't need it."

They rode some more in silence as they walked the horses over the long rolling hump of prairie expanse.

"You know how I did it?" Davy asked, eager to explain what he had just discovered. "I thought of that jackrabbit out back in town. He was on the run, and I got him. Just like that Korpec guy back there. He was a jackrabbit, that's all. And I got him. I knew the split second I pulled the trigger that I had him."

They listened to the echo of Davy's words in their ears. " 'What fools these mortals be,' " Doc said finally, smiling at the kid.

"What's that supposed to mean?"

"I didn't say it. Somebody else did. Don't blame me. I'm only along for the ride."

"Yeah."

They rode into the double canyon junction that led to Scarecrow.

"It's easy, isn't it?" Davy said. "I mean, when you get over it, it's really easy."

Jack shook his head.

"But it is."

Doc glanced at Jack, and together they watched Davy lift his gun hand to the horizon, point his two first fingers as he would a gun barrel, and follow the imaginary jackrabbit running scared in front of him.

They trotted into Scarecrow, boarded their horses at the livery, and headed straight for the hotel to eat. Two men were already eating at one of the tables. The Mexican woman studied Jack, Doc, and Davy as they walked in, her face full of questions about what happened at Lee's Mine. *"Buenos,"* she said.

"Buenos," Jack returned.

They sat down, and when she came to their table they ordered a plate of Mexican food and beer.

"Encuentraste Lee's Mine?" she asked, but the real question was, what happened?

"Si," Jack said, "we found it. Your directons were good. *Gracias."*

She waited, a tentative look of apprehension on her face.

"It turned out all right," Jack said to satisfy her.

"We're alive," Doc added.

Davy looked from one to the other, waiting for more, his face like a hungry dog upturned for its daily bone. He couldn't keep it in. "A *lot* happened."

The woman looked to Davy for an explanation. *"Que paso?"*

Davy looked to Jack for translation.

"What happened?" he said, and glanced at Doc with tolerance.

"Lee's Mine was all right," he said to the woman. "I mean, I got to see my brother and we talked things out. Nothing happened there, I guess. But later, that's when we got ambushed."

The woman fixed her eyes on Davy's. She shook her head. *"No es bueno,* the ambush," she said.

The two men on the other side of the room were eavesdropping, forks midair. Davy glanced over at them and back to the woman. "They had us surrounded, almost," he went on, his voice louder this time. "We were riding through this canyon, and they started shooting. I heard the shots whistling by my head. We ran for cover and planned what to do. They had us pinned down, all right. We didn't know who they were at first, but then we figured it out. There were four of them—and just the three of us." He paused to let the odds set in.

Jack half turned in his chair to wait for Davy to finish. Doc inhaled and exhaled loudly.

Davy missed their messages. "They circled in on us," he continued, "and they thought they had us because they outnumbered us, but we had our own plan. Jack went one way and Doc the other, and I stayed in one place. That way they had to focus on three different places instead of one. We covered each other when we moved in on them. We turned the circle back on them." He glanced at the two men watching from the next table.

The woman stood impassive in front of Davy; it was obvious she didn't understand half of what he was saying.

"It was really risky," he went on. "I mean, *really* risky. Lots of shooting. I thought I was going to get hit a couple times, but I just kept shooting. I had to reload three times. Then they started going after Jack—all four of them because we were separated now. But Doc and I kept them quiet, didn't we?"

Doc nodded and said, "We sneaked up to them and stuffed rags in their mouths."

Davy paid no attenton. "So there we were," he said. "Three against four of them. Then one guy went really crazy, like he didn't care anything about anything. He closed in on Jack. Jack was up behind some boulders, and the other guys were firing and keeping him down. Doc and I, we were just blasting away at them, but this one killer ran straight at Jack, firing away. That's when I trained on him, because I knew I had to stop him. So I took careful aim and fired. I missed; he was running in and out so fast, and he was farther away than it looked. I fired again, and stopped him right in his tracks. I had to. Otherwise, he would have gotten Jack."

The woman stood motionless, her arms folded, showing concern as though this seventeen-year-old were her own son.

Davy glanced at the listening strangers. Then he looked at Jack and Doc, both of them eyeing Davy with extravagant tolerance.

"You start pinning medals on yourself," Jack said, "and pretty soon they turn into targets."

After they finished eating, Davy stood up and asked, "Come out back, will you? I need your advice."

They followed Davy through the back door of the hotel, walked past the outbuildng, and stepped through the weeds. They watched the kid loosen his gun in his holster and plant his boots ready in the slippery earth.

"I just want to know if I'm doing this right," he said. "I want to get better."

"So you can kill jackrabbits on the second shot?" Jack asked.

"No. I mean, anything can happen. Look what happened today."

"Davy boy," Doc said, "that was an exception. You know why that happened, and it wasn't because of you."

"But that's just it. The exception is what you have to look out for, isn't it?"

Neither of them said anything. They knew Davy called them out there not for advice but for him to show them what he could do.

So Davy whipped out his gun one time after another, each time asking Jack and Doc if he was doing it the best way possible, the fastest possible. What were their secrets? How could he cut down the time? Should he tie his holster higher or lower? How should he hold his hand?

Then he pointed to a rock, drew, and fired. He hit it. Was there a faster way? Was that the way they would do it?

He drew and fired again. How often did they practice?

Would they shoot the way he did? Is it better to overaim or underaim?

Telling brave tales in a safe hotel was one side of guns. That alone could get anyone into trouble. Bragging had a magnetism that drew out the gunslinging bugs from the walls to shoot down the braggers, to eliminate the competition. But Jack knew that self-deception could have a worse effect. An inflated talent—a fast technique—was less than half the force behind a gun. This kind of self-deception could push a man to his gun sooner than necessary, and if the situation was unlucky, the gunman was dead. That was the seed Jack saw growing in Davy.

The next morning, the woman said, *"Buenos dias,"* and held out an envelope. *"Señor* Jack?"

"Buenos dias," he said. *"Sí."*

"Para usted esta vez."

"Gracias." He took the envelope, opened it, and read the message twice.

"What is it?" Doc asked. Jack handed him the note:

> *Your woman is good as dead.*
> *Korpec*

CHAPTER 16

DOC stuffed the note in his jacket pocket. "Let's go."

He and Jack headed for the door. "Hey!" Davy called, standing alone with his mouth open. "What's going on?"

"*Señor?*" the Mexican woman asked. "Do you wish *comida* ?"

Doc said over his shoulder, "No, *señora. Gracias.* We aren't hungry." Then he walked with Jack through the door and headed to the livery on the outskirts of town.

Davy followed them out the hotel, skipping along the boardwalk to catch up. "What's the matter?"

Jack ignored him.

When Davy asked Doc, he got the same reaction. Suddenly, Davy was in the periphery, and he knew it. He hurried to keep up, studying their faces for a clue to this abrupt change in status, with no invitation to speak. They didn't answer his questions. They didn't acknowledge his presence.

The air around Jack gave off an electric charge of danger. The way he rushed with a heightened alertness on a hair trigger broadcast the message: Do not disturb, do not intrude, maintain the distance.

They stepped off the boardwalk at the corner of the third building. Still, Jack said nothing. Doc matched his stride in the same determined, straight-path rhythm that signaled to anyone with any sense that these men were not to be approached.

All Davy could do was to move along, half-skip now and then to keep up, like an untrained colt. He knew enough not to ask anything yet.

They saddled their horses, mounted, and rode out the main road through town, turning south at the outskirts.

Davy rode along as he was expected. "Where we headed?"

"Caliente," Doc said, reaching into his jacket pocket and pulling out the piece of paper. He handed it across to Davy.

The kid read the note.

Jack rode with his jaw set tight, his eyes straight ahead. He moved his horse at a fast walk, making headway but not exhausting the animal too soon. The balance between reality and imagination held to its fulcrum in him for the long ride back to Caliente. He had to accept that his vision couldn't be obliterated through unreined anger to get there before Korpec and his men. His desire to protect Linda had to be checked. His control against the pressure to kick spurs at the infinite distance to Caliente was the very defense that made Jack who he was.

The three rode over the low-shadowed terrain, the buttes and mesas casting their eclipses to the west as the sun rose.

Davy was lost to the territory they rode through. The day before, he had been the center of attention. Now he trailed along like a pack mule. But he knew when to hold his tongue, and so did Doc.

They rode in silence for miles on end, the heat of the day wavering in a distant mirage on the semidesert. They were isolated in the vastness of country, and they rode equidistant from each other.

They were lucky. The water hole flowed enough for themselves and their horses. The cottonwoods shielded them from the high sun and filtered the air through the shadowy branches.

They sat against the trunks of individual trees and waited through the midday broil.

Jack was the first to see the movement of a rider on the

horizon. Then Doc. Davy noticed long after he realized that the two intense men with him had become motionless and hunter alert.

The hazy figure grew like a tiny reed vibrating in the background haze, slowly enlarging. The rider headed straight for the cottonwood spring, no stranger to its location, and judging from the day, needing it.

Jack watched without a shift of his body, analyzing the figure before the rider could be deciphered up close, studying him, waiting for details to surface. The rider made steady progress toward the spring, moderating the pace of his horse against the terrain, angle of sun, and distance from the water hole.

In a few minutes, the shape of man and horse enlarged to include the outline curvatures and limits, although the atmosphere still shimmered the figure in and out of focus.

More minutes and the colors appeared with resolution, although these, too, melted into each other—the brown of the horse, the black-green of the man's torso.

Finally, the rider was close enough for Jack to figure that he could see the three of them waiting and watching under the cotonwoods. That was when the rider slowed his progress, a precaution more than a natural reaction. Seeing three men crouched to the ground could mean a setup. The lone rider proceeded at a calculating pace and with caution.

Jack knew that the rider had a line of vision above the groundline where the three of them lay. That extra height on his horse gave him the advantage.

The rider emerged from the shimmering heat, and his silhouette sharpened as though he had passed through glass. Fifty feet away, he reined in and sat in his saddle, studying the scene.

Jack turned to Doc and asked the wordless question of whether he finally recognized the man. Doc smiled and nodded.

The man sat with one hand on his saddlehorn, the other near his gun, studying the three of them in return. He was a big man, deep-skinned from range riding, his broad-brimmed sombrero shadowing his eyes so he could see against the glare of the sun, his bushy mustache drooping down his cheeks and jaw. The shirt turned out to be green and tan, not black. He was one with his horse, rifle ready at the side, lariat, canteen, saddlebags, bedroll all compact and efficiently placed.

The man was in no hurry. A minute passed before he was sure. Only then did he call out, "That you, Jack?"

Jack stood up. "Rab?"

"That you, Doc?"

Doc stood up and replied, "It's not Aristotle."

"Yeah, that's you. Who's the other one?"

Davy stood up on cue, but Jack merely shouted, "A friend."

Rab moved his horse toward the shade and water.

Jack turned to Davy and with a hushed, unmistakable command, he said, "We'll do the talking." His eyes locked on Davy's, the message plain that what he said he meant. "That's Rab Wood," he added. "U.S. marshal."

Davy nodded, glancing at the marshal riding in at a walk.

They waited as Rab closed the distance and stopped in front of them. He remained in the saddle longer than anyone else normally would, glancing down at Davy more than usual besides. This was a very cautious man, one who still was assessing whether Jack and Doc were free agents or were held in tow somehow by the one he didn't know.

Satisfied, Rab dismounted, his eyes still more on Davy.

"Good to see you," Jack said, stepping forward, stretching his hand and shaking it with the marshal.

"What the hell you doing out here?" Rab asked. "I thought only prairie dogs knew what they were doing in this godforsaken country."

"I was going to ask you the same thing."

"Well, I'm heading north. Got sidetracked. Some loco shooting business up in Leisure City, that old dump."

"Sounds to me like you're going up for some cards," Doc said. "I know Leisure City. It won me half a year's living last time I rode through."

"Guess that's why they call it Leisure City."

"I guess so."

Rab led his horse to the water, took off his hat, and wiped the sweat from his forehead with his forearm. "Where you headed?"

"Caliente," Jack said.

Rab drank some water, splashed it on his neck and face. "Riding north pretty much, huh?" he asked, the question a roundabout intrusion that friends used.

"Pretty much. We're looking for Davy's brother."

Rab glanced at the kid. "I heard," he said, and stood up.

Doc leaned back against the cottonwood. "We've covered quite a spread. It was like freshman year in the University of the West."

Rab didn't smile. "Did you find him?" he asked Davy point-blank.

Davy glanced at Jack and hesitated enough to show that he was finding out that Rab wasn't one to smokescreen with a story. He nodded. "Back there out of Scarecrow. We just talked. I haven't seen him in a long time. I wanted to find out what was going on."

"Did you?"

"Yeah."

"That where he is now? Scarecrow?"

Jack took the focus. "No, he rode out someplace. Haven't heard anything since."

"Don't know where or when?"

"He just rode away. Who knows where?"

"East?"

"Yeah, east. But he could be anywhere now. I didn't ask."

Rab turned back to the kid. "I think he's on the dodge. He's wanted. You know that?"

Davy nodded.

"Well, I got other things to do," Rab said, looking at Jack and shrugging. "Like getting me some water."

The three of them watched the marshal drink more, soak his kerchief, wipe his neck with it, fill his canteen. Nothing else was said of Sam Bates.

The men talked of the towns that were growing, like Halfway, and the ones that were dying, like Scarecrow, except the proportion of people wasn't, only shifting in location. New people were moving west in droves and crowding in. Some of the wagon trains were interfering with cattle trails and ranges, cluttering up the country with too many brothers and sisters and leaving their debris and houses and boom-and-bust towns all over the landscape.

"Change is trouble," Doc said. "That's my considered opinion. We need to lock the gates, now that we're in, of course. No change, no trouble. Of course, that would put you out of a job."

"Then we got to keep the gates open," Rab said with no smile. He paused and glanced at Davy and then over at Jack. "You talk to Zeke at Halfway? Korpec's passing word on you."

"Yeah, I know. Zeke told me."

"You know where he is?"

Jack shook his head. "Riding somewhere. He'll ride out the steam."

"He might. I'd keep an eye out. Word spreads. I picked it up."

"That can't be helped."

"You know where he is? Korpec? Where he's headed?"

Jack looked to the endless country beyond the cotton-woods and spread the palm of his hand to the horizon. "He could be anywhere."

Rab paused and then said, "I did a hanging two months ago in Jeremy. You know it?"

Jack nodded. "New Mexico."

"A man shot a blacksmith and stole his horse. Left a widow and three kids."

Running into Rab Wood was what Jack needed. When the marshal rode north and the three of them headed south, Jack had regained the better part of his equilibrium and lost his high-strung tension. He was forced to talk to Rab, forced to act as if nothing had happened with Korpec. He wanted no interference from the marshal. He wanted to handle Korpec on his own.

The crimped edges of his eyes disappeared. The looseness in his arms returned. He kept the same sensible steady pace south, still restraining the urge to speed home, knowing that a surge of fast riding only spelled disaster to the animals and more agony and delay in not getting to Caliente faster.

What was more, he could be talked to. After they had ridden half an hour, Davy asked, "Do you think Rab knows about Korpec? I mean, what happened?"

"No."

"It sounded like he did."

"Davy boy," Doc said, "you got to realize that the difference between a U.S. marshal and a thieving, no-good snake in the grass is"—he held up his thumb and forefinger with an inch between—"about that much. They have the same conniving minds, except that one wears the badge and the other one doesn't. Rab Wood is after other game."

"My brother? Is the marshal good with a gun?"

"One time I saw him in the Flat Iron saloon clean out some drinking cowhands," Jack said. "They were making some trouble and fighting. He came in and told them to clear out. When one of the drunks raised a bottle over his head to come at him, Rab whipped out his gun faster than anybody could see and shot the bottle out of his hand. The glass spattered, and half the whiskey fell on the drunk's head.

That was one scared, quiet saloon. Yeah, he knows how to use it."

Doc laughed. "Remember that rodeo in White River? He had ten shots to pick off ten bottles. Someone got eight. Rab got ten."

"Maybe you saw the Bowie in his boot," Jack said to Davy, "but you didn't see the Derringer in his side pocket."

"He rules with iron, so to speak," Doc said. "Yes, I'd say Rab Wood prefers bull's-eyes to bullshit. There aren't many who fear nothing but God. He's one of them."

They rode along the top of a mammoth uplift of earth. It telescoped a vantage point to the land that flowed around them fifty miles in all directions. The deceiving distance was bordered by an edge of mesas in an irregular pattern on the horizon.

"We'll kill Korpec," Davy said out of the blue. "He doesn't have that much headstart. Maybe he left that note in the morning."

"He didn't," Jack said. "He left it at night."

"How do you know that?"

"Because I know Korpec."

"That still doesn't give him much of a lead."

"We could be following right on their tracks," Doc said. "Right in front of us."

At sundown, they stopped at another water hole. Davy wanted to know how they knew about it, but Jack and Doc went about the business of watering the horses and drinking. They rested in the fading yellow-orange light and ate hardtack and jerky.

Davy stood up and unlashed his saddle roll. Jack told him to put it back; they weren't camping.

They mounted up and rode in the moonlight. The three-quarter moon washed the open land with more than enough light. They rode through a changed terrain, shadowy and eerie in its range of muted grays and blacks. The country was the same, but the cooler, still air and the night awakened a different alertness in them. The silhouettes of the land they were accustomed to seeing took on a transformed aggression that made them turn their heads more, be more watchful, quicker to respond to the slightest unaccountable noise.

The alien hour shortened their horizons, but their impulse to keep moving increased their guard and anticipation. The expectation of catching up to Korpec and his men fed the night-light of their imaginations, kept them quiet, kept them wary.

They rode the night hours that half blinded their horizons until they crested the bluff that revealed the outline of ragged black rectangles scattered from the core of the town. Candles and kerosene lamps glowed from some of the buildings. The town was a derelict to the night, an ambivalence. Doc knew, of course, but for Davy's benefit Jack identified the town as Willow Springs.

CHAPTER 17

WHEN they approached the town, they spotted the saloon from the light pouring from it, more than from any other building. Moonlight reflected off the structures in a strange, gluey veneer, but the lights from the saloon had a heated yellow glow to them.

The hotel was at the east end of Willow Springs, but Jack led them down the slope and wide around the last building set back from the road. The building was abandoned, or whoever was inside was already sleeping. No sign of horse, barn, water trough, nothing but what was useful to someone who didn't care about necessities.

They rode past three more buildings, two of them houses, one a storage shed with broken slats and the swing door open. The next house they passed was built close to the road. Someone parted a curtain on the front window and held it steady until they passed. The curtain was opened too far to mean anything but curiosity.

The closer to the center, the more scattered lights shone through the windows, some of them curtained, some bare. The stores were closed—the clothier, the general store, tools and guns, restaurant. No newspaper, no bank, no sheriff. This was a town that filled in the space between other towns, the kind of unkempt settlement that grew where it was because the distance between the others was called for, as if nature decreed that Willow Springs should be exactly there, just as nature did with the distance between pine trees and rabbit warrens.

They continued easy down the center of the road, the buildings with false fronts on both sides. Some were connected, some separated by alleys, some isolated on purpose with plenty of riding and seeing space between. No one walked the boardwalks, no one sat outside, leaving the town a ghostlike shell of listening walls and watching windows. The signs on the stores were the only voices.

Ordinarily, the light and noise at the hotel saloon would have been a beacon of rest out of the tiring night, and partially it was that. But the specter of Max Korpec and his men on the run toward Caliente, and with the declared vow to kill Linda, tarnished the glow. Still, they headed toward the only concentration of light on the road, their heads turning left and right at the darkened corners and passageways of the buildings.

A dog barked once far behind them. The yelp had a disquieting, disembodied presence to it, its sound disintegrating fast in the open night. Davy turned around, pausing longer than necessary because he couldn't locate the dog.

They approached the hotel saloon. The light shone through the front windows on either side of the batwing doors, casting elongated rectangles across the boardwalk and into the road. Compared with the rest of the town, this looked like the place where some human noise would be emerging, but it didn't. The saloon was a voiceless lighted room out of joint with itself for all its welcoming facade in the night.

Jack led the way toward the hitching post. The three of them were tired and needed a rest. It was a long day, and longer days loomed ahead.

A man stepped through the swinging door and stopped on the boardwalk.

The timing was all the more startling because no hint of anyone inside had come from the saloon. Most of the light came from behind the man, shadowing his face, but the slight halting step he made was a sign that he hadn't expected anyone. The man was merely stepping outside for some air or to be alone or to see whatever the town looked like in the middle of nowhere.

The three of them paid little attention after the first reaction. They rode the few paces to the post—into the light.

The man on the boardwalk froze in his tracks. His stance showed more than surprise or deliberation or vigilance. He was struck by recognition, and for the time it took for him to loosen the grip that locked his body, he revealed the danger that he represented.

Jack was second in that recognition. The light was against him, showing his face but blocking the stranger's.

The man drew first.

Jack drew.

The man fired and backed into the saloon. The shot thundered into the midnight calm, shattering the silence and, it seemed, even the night-darkened buildings.

Jack fired back, but his horse balked with the man's shot.

The night unthreaded into turmoil. Doc drew and fired from his saddle. Davy reined his horse steady, but it lunged and bucked to escape; he drew and fired, a useless shot through the doors.

"Korpec!" Jack shouted, yanking his roan and spurring it. "Come on!"

Doc followed, but Davy was slow to react, looking at the two of them riding away, looking to the door, and finally riding after them.

Jack and Doc stopped three buildings down, dismounted on the run, and sped into the alley, Davy following. "What's he doing here?" the kid asked. "Are you sure that's him?"

"The other two are in there," Jack said, his face hardened as it was in Scarecrow that morning. "They're not going to split up."

Doc pulled Davy out of sight by the scruff of his neck. "Get in here."

Jack peered around the corner.

"We caught up to them," Davy said of the obvious. "What'll we do?"

When Jack pulled back, he studied Davy and whispered with the force of an order. "Use your head."

"We have to split up," Doc said, the quickness in his voice underlying what Jack already knew: Korpec and his men were running in different directions down the street.

Jack leaned around the corner again, studying the buildings, the distance between them and the saloon, the obstacles and protections. He nodded. "They're going out the back to get out of the light."

Doc looked behind them down the alley. "We're sitting ducks here, Jack."

"Let's get to the other side. Cover me." Jack set himself ready. He looked over his shoulder at Davy. "You go next." He glanced at Doc with the understanding that he didn't want the kid to panic, and he relied on Doc to get Davy across the road and out of the alley.

Jack sprinted into the open, running through the shadows, his boots on the hard earth. He disappeared into the black alley on the slight diagonal, the darkness eclipsing him like a slice of night.

A few seconds later, Davy ran the same way and lunged into the darkness next to Jack. He pressed himself against the building, his breath heaving, his head tilted up.

"Over there." Jack pointed with the barrel of his gun to the opposite side. "Cover Doc."

Davy stepped across and leaned against the other building, his gun aimed high.

They waited for the seconds to pass. Suddenly, Doc appeared as a blur, the only wash of movement against the solidity of the buildings. He ran straight toward Jack and Davy.

Shots blasted their thunder through the night, reverberating down the tunnel of the alley across the road, the same alley the three of them had escaped. Three shots. Four. And five.

Jack stuck out his Colt, but Doc was weaving in and out and blocking the sight line to the alley.

Then he raised his gun and fired off four shots into the air, the only weapon left to fend off the attack by fear and intimidation. Davy did the same.

Doc dove between Jack and Davy. Only then did the two of them empty their guns into the lightless alley that they had just escaped.

They leaned back against the walls and reloaded fast, jamming shells into the chambers. "You all right?" Jack asked.

"Yeah," Doc said, gasping for air. "They almost had dead duck for dinner."

Jack peered out across the road. "They aren't going to stay there, and we're not staying here."

Doc got to his feet. "Maybe that's what they're figuring too."

"Yeah," Jack said, calculating fast. "I'll stay. They'll be coming after us. You two let them know we've split up."

Doc nodded once.

"You can do this?" Jack asked Davy.

"Yeah, sure."

"Don't panic. You stay between us."

Davy nodded fast.

"You hear me," Jack hissed, his eyes branding the message into the kid. Valuable time was wasting. "Get over to the next alley. Doc is going down to the one after that."

Davy nodded again in obedience.

Doc punched Davy's arm. "Let's go."

They ran down the alley to the rear of the buildings, checked their safety at the end, and slipped around to the next two alleys.

Jack pictured them in his mind as they separated at the end of the building, Davy moving up toward the front of the buildings and the main road, Doc running down to the next alley and stationing himself at its front too. The three of them waited in the cracks of the town for Korpec to make the move.

A new silence took root, an ominous black flower of the night.

When Jack heard the boot scuffing behind him, he whirled around. The flimsy crunching sound funneled down the length of the alley, carried by the narrow walls. In the open, the noise would have dispersed without a trace.

The gibbous moon poured over the rooftops and slipped into the alleys. But beyond the buildings the light was inescapable, and it brushed over the figure at the end of the alley—and glinted off gun metal.

Jack squatted to the ground. The man fired and missed, his shot marred by the movement. He ran to the rear shadow of the building.

The man—maybe Korpec, maybe one of his gang—had run the length of the other side of town and crept along the rear of the buildings, checking the alleys as he went, trying to flush them out.

The shouts alerted everyone and ignited a flurry of bullets back and forth across the main road, the lighting of gunfire locating the shooters like giant flint sparks in the dark.

Two men stationed themselves on either end of the porch of the general store, one behind a pile of grain sacks, the other behind a stack of lumber. They fired three rounds at Doc and Davy, who returned the fire.

Jack fired at an angle, forcing them behind their cover and establishing where he was. Then he ran down the alley after the one he'd missed, eased around, and along the rear building away from Davy and Doc.

The man could be anywhere, but chances were that he'd headed back around the building and toward the main road. Jack crouched low to the corner, looked around, saw no one.

He ran down the alley, past a galvanized tank and water barrels, stopped at the corner, and listened. Nothing.

The two at the store slipped back into the alleys on the other side. Davy fired once, but Doc knew better.

The men were going to circle around and try to outflank Doc and Davy.

But Doc had abandoned his alley and run along the front of the main road to the second alley beyond Davy, changing his location and leaving an alley between the kid and him.

The man Jack trailed had escaped. Either he was hiding behind the jumble of tossed-out furniture at the entrance or he'd discovered that Jack was no longer where he'd left him. Either way, the killer was sure to find Davy.

With each catlike step, Jack tested the boardwalk for the creaks it might give. Gun ready, he moved close to the front of the restaurant, and banked on the other two being out of sight behind the other row of buildings across the road. In a quick move, he cleared the corner. But the alley was empty.

The man was making a figure eight of the buildings. It was clear—he knew where Davy was and that Doc had run down to another building.

Jack moved to the front of the building again, but it was too late.

The man already edged along the far building toward Doc.

Davy still fired across the road, where the other two answered his fire.

Shouting at the kid was the wrong move. Jack tiptoed toward them.

Then all hell broke loose. The man zeroed in on Doc.

Davy saw the raised arm out the corner of his eye, and turned.

The killer heard Davy's boots behind him. The sound jumped his gun hand enough so that he was caught between them.

Davy froze.

The man saw his chance as he whirled on his own panic. Doc had to be killed first, not the kid. He turned back fast and fired the instant Doc realized the interplay of Davy and the killer and his own death.

The wild shot clipped Doc off his legs.

The man turned back to kill Davy.

And Davy stood with panic still in his eyes, immobilized in a surrender of will and life.

Doc fired from the ground. The bullet exploded through the man's back and lungs and heart, sending the man in a screamless terror straight at Davy until the body smashed against the boardwalk skull first.

In the midst of it all, a second killer charged diagonally from behind Jack. He ran low across the road, his gun leading the way, leveled at Jack and firing once, twice, three times.

Jack crouched and fired twice, the gap between them closing.

Jack's third shot kicked and twisted the man once and dropped him to the dirt like a bundle of bricks. And the silence that followed was total, the contrast immense from the moments of gunfire.

One more killer was left. Jack shoved his hand backward at Davy to get back.

He rushed into the shadows himself and waited.

Nothing.

Then, finally, they heard the sound of hooves beyond the buildings. The muffled clopping faded to the darkness as the sound wove through the stores and houses and then deadened to the distance.

Jack ran over to Doc while Davy pressed himself tight out of sight, frightened and ashamed of what he had done. "You all right?"

Doc winced, his hand on his leg. "Who'd I get?"

"Are you all right?" Jack repeated.

"Yeah."

Jack turned the man over on the boardwalk and rolled him back faceup. Then he walked to the man in the road facing straight up. He went back to Doc. "It's Korpec."

CHAPTER 18

WHILE Davy stood over Doc, Jack pulled the kerchief from his neck. "Where'd it get you?"

"I'm all right. It just grazed my thigh." He twisted to his side to stand up.

Jack pushed him back down. "Wait. Let me see."

"Nothing's broken. It just grazed me, that's all."

"That's enough. Hold his pants leg, Davy."

The kid stayed put, staring down at Doc.

"Hey!"

The chagrin and pain of what Davy had not done kept him immobilized again, this time staring at Doc lying wounded in the alley dirt. It was the kid's fault, and too late to do anything about what happened.

"Davy, get the hell down here and help me."

Finally, he crouched down, avoiding Doc's eyes as much as he could until it was impossible. He saw Jack pressing his kerchief against Doc's thigh. To see the man on the ground locked him tight again. He stood up and stared.

"It's nothing," Doc said, "but it sure burned like hell. It probably branded itself closed, probably not even bleeding."

"It's bleeding," Jack said, and looked up at Davy. "Get down here and hold his pants tight. I'm going to cut it open and see what's going on."

"Some Stoic said something brilliant for times like this," Doc said, "but I don't know what it is." He caught Davy's reticence. "It's all right, Davy boy," he said, smiling. "Zeus just threw me a thunderbolt, that's all."

"Hold it here," Jack said, taking his knife from its sheath.

Davy grabbed the pants leg and stretched it tight against

143

the thigh. Jack angled the long-bladed knife in and away from Doc's leg, slashing the denim open, exposing the wound. Doc half sat up to join the other two staring at the red rip in his flesh.

"What'd I tell you?"

"Yeah, yeah," Jack said. "Big hero."

"It's not even bleeding."

"The hell it isn't. You're bleeding all over Willow Springs."

Doc winced as Jack wiped the blood leaking from the wound, dabbing and smoothing it clean. "You son of a bitch," he said, "ruining my kerchief. Now I have to buy a new one."

"Next time get a red one," Doc said. "What about me? I have to buy a new pair of pants."

"What for? There's nothing wrong with these," Jack said, pressing the kerchief onto the wound, stopping the blood seeping out the gash.

"You ruined them."

"I'm thinking of cutting off your leg next," Jack said. "Amputating the whole damn thing. It'll do you good."

Davy was too quiet. He knelt beside Doc but hunched his shoulders in repugnance of what he was forced to see and think. The pain was all the more poigant as the two friends jabbed and bantered with each other.

"I'm sorry," Davy said.

Doc reached up and slapped the back of his fingers on the kid's shoulder. "Don't worry, I'm all right. Jack's having fun with his knife. He always wanted to be a butcher."

"Get it out of your head," Jack told Davy. "We all make mistakes."

"Come on," Doc said, propping himself up on his elbow. "It's time for some Lydia Pinkham all-purpose elixir."

Jack pushed him back down. "Wait, hero. I'm going to tie it up." He held out his hand to Davy. "I need your kerchief."

Davy already had it off his neck. Jack tied the two kerchiefs together, smoothed them over the wound, wrapped the ends around Doc's leg, and knotted them tight.

"Thanks, Doc."

Jack and Davy took each arm and lifted him to his feet. "All right?"

Doc nodded. "It's nothing."

"I know."

Doc laughed and put the first pressure of a step on his leg. He pursed his lips. "Yeah, it's all right. Where's the whiskey? I got to replenish all the blood I lost."

"Yeah, yeah."

They walked toward the saloon. One by one the townspeople emerged from the buildings. A few were wearing nightshirts. Some stook on the edge of the boardwalks, some in the road. They kept their distance, watching, testing the scene to see if all the shooting and fighting were over. The ones who stood in twos and threes talked back and forth but couldn't be heard.

Doc favored the leg as they went, limping and leaning on the two of them on either side. Davy was the only one who looked down at what was left of Max Korpec dead in the road. They walked past as if Doc had snagged himself on a nail. A few inches more and the shot would have killed him.

When Jack and Davy helped Doc up the stairs of the saloon, some of the men ran out to collect the bodies, keeping their distance from the three men as they went, making wide arcs around them.

Inside, Jack forced Doc onto a long bench against a side wall. The proprietor brought some soft cotton cloth and a bowl of water from the kitchen; he said he hadn't any hot water ready at this time of night; he was heating some up.

Jack untied the kerchiefs and wiped the wound clean again in the light. When the hot water came, he did it again. In the light, he could see that the ball had torn the skin and some muscle. It was a flesh wound; no bones shattered or lead inside.

"Do you have any Lydia Pinkham stuff?" he asked the proprietor.

"This ain't no infirmary," the man said.

"Damn," Doc said jokingly. "Guess I'll have to go for whiskey."

Jack uncorked the bottle, poured the glass half full, and handed it to Doc, who propped himself up to take the glass. But before Doc took it, Jack poured it on the wound.

Doc gritted his teeth and muttered at the sizzling pain of the disinfecting alcohol. "Goddamn," he said, "what a son-of-a-bitch friend you are."

The next morning, at breakfast, again Davy said, "I'm sorry for what happened."

"Davy boy, forget it. It turned out all right, didn't it?"

He nodded.

"So that's what counts."

Davy paused and shook his head. "It isn't. I didn't come through, when I should have."

"Sure you did. If you hadn't seen the bastard, he would've killed me. I wouldn't have had a chance. You gave me a chance. I should be thanking you."

It was an elaborate rationalization, and Davy knew it. He smiled at the generous lie. "I don't know," he said, and looked down at his hands on the table. "I panicked. Just what I said I wouldn't do."

"We all do." Doc said, and slapped the kid on the shoulder. "We all panic."

"You don't. And I didn't back at Scarecrow."

Jack leaned into the conversation. "Because they were too far away there."

Davy didn't understand.

"There's a difference between someone firing at you at a hundred feet and ten feet. Up close they're human, and you don't want to get shot."

Davy waited and listened.

"So you froze because you realized you were aiming at a man, not just a target. Only, you forgot that he was out to kill you, no matter what. To him, you *were* a target. Nothing you could do about that. He was out to kill you and the two of us besides."

"Davy boy," Doc said, "the difference between firing on a scared rabbit and a killer with eyes so close you can see them is the difference between sunup and sundown. It changes the direction of everything. It's something you have to get used to."

Davy hung his head. "I still feel bad. I should've pulled the trigger. That's all it took. Just a squeeze on the trigger and it wouldn't have happened."

"Don't dwell on it," Jack said.

"I can't help it. You won't trust me anymore. You won't think I can handle anything. Well, I can. I know I can."

"We know that."

"Then why did I freeze up?"

They didn't answer.

Davy looked from one to the other. "Because I was scared," he answered for them.

"We all get scared," Jack said.

"But it almost cost us our lives. He could've shot me, only he went after you first. I just stood there. I can't believe I did that. It happened so fast. All of a sudden, I saw him and he saw me and then he turned around and shot you. Why didn't I get him then? I had the perfect chance, right there in front of him. Only, I didn't."

"He was a lousy shot," Doc said, and smiled. Davy had to smile back and shake his head.

The three of them laughed. "I'll tell you one thing," Davy said, his face changing. "That'll never happen again." He looked from Doc to Jack and back again to Doc. "I swear. I'll never lose my nerve again. Never."

They stayed in Willow Springs three days. The townspeople kept their distance, letting the three strangers alone after realizing soon enough that they posed no further harm or threat. The feud between them and the Korpec gang wasn't their concern if it stopped right there. Word got out who the two dead men were. The fact that Korpec was wanted for robbery and murder stamped approval on what Jack, Doc, and Davy had done and even resulted now and then in respect and admiration. No town wanted killers passing through, especially when the town wasn't large enough for a sheriff.

On the second afternoon, a stranger came to the three of them and said he'd heard about how it all happened. He was glad of it. He didn't know who those men were, but something about them he didn't like. Now he knew. He invited Jack and his friends to stay in Willow Springs for as long as they liked.

Doc outfitted himself with a new pair of denims, all the time making an extravagant display of anguish over the loss of his old pair. He made loud complaints about how stiff the cloth was, how foreign and starched they felt on his legs, especially against the wound. It was worse by the minute because of these new pants. How would Jack Tyson feel when Doc got the chance to reverse the situation? he asked. When he could plunge his own long-bladed knife into Jack's shirt and pants, slicing them up to rags just for a ghoulish look at a wound so minor that no scar worth its salt would consider showing itself?

After this palaver of mock self-pity, they took their time refilling their cartridge belts and saddlebags, cleaning their guns and rifles, checking on their horses at the livery for new shoes and feed.

On the third morning, they mounted up and rode out of town. Jack and Davy tried time and again to solicit the truth about Doc's leg. Doc insisted it was all right, and it seemed to be. The surface wound healed fast.

With Korpec out of their minds, they moseyed along, their spirits at ease with the world, the hurry and anger in them left behind in Willow Springs.

Doc turned to Davy and said that he probably didn't notice but Jack was thinking about something else besides beans and rice in Caliente. Ah, yes, something quite different. And Doc got Davy to look at Jack and smile, because it finally dawned on the kid that he was talking about Linda.

Jack smiled back, playing the role of trapped and exposed partner, someone known too much by a friend. And Davy said, Oh, yeah, that was it, wasn't it? Jack said nothing, as he always did about such matters, but Doc wouldn't let him get away with that too fast. He plied a few more discomforts upon Jack and got Davy to add his own.

They rode with Caliente in mind, home where they could rest among friends and take their time through the days. The attraction of familiar people and places kept them on a steady pace south where they knew they'd be welcomed and celebrated for their return. The prospect of Caliente was one of solace and cheer after the long haul on body and soul.

CHAPTER 19

JACK, Doc, and Davy couldn't hear what they were seeing yet, but the sight of activity drew them on, their destination now before their eyes.

Weaving through the sage, creosote, and ocotillo brought them to the north road, rutted from wagon wheels and trampled by horses into a straight trail in and out of town. A lone man in a buckboard poked along toward them. They moved aside as the buckboard approached, banging and clanking under the hot sun. The driver nodded and raised his reins in greeting as the riders passed. He was hauling fence posts on the back. The wheels churned up noonday dust. He moved past them without a word, because he didn't recognize the riders; his rifle rested beside him on the seat.

At the junction of the north and west roads, they turned to the east and followed the road that led directly past Linda's house on the outskirts of town.

When they approached her house, Doc said, "Well, Davy boy, how about the two of us getting ourselves a drink and some victuals?"

"Sure. What about Jack?"

"Jack'll be along. He's got some things to do."

"Oh, yeah," Davy said, glancing at Linda's house and back to Jack.

"We'll take our poor, tired, lonely selves up to the Road's End and meet you later."

"How much later?" Davy asked, grinning.

"That's a good question," Doc said. "It might be later today, or for all anybody knows next week. We'll just go our lonely way and drown ourselves in demon drink. We'll do our best."

"You're breaking my heart," Jack told him.

"You see, Davy boy, he's got his time all accounted for and, sorry to say, we're not included."

Doc and Davy were going to ride right on past while Jack pulled reins, got off, knocked on the door, and hoped Linda was there. But before they could get there, Linda opened the door and hurried down the boardwalk, her face bright and welcoming, her man returned. She waved and called out, "Jack!"

She rushed to him as Jack dismounted and flung her arms around him. "I'm so glad to see you!"

Doc and Davy watched. Then Doc slapped Davy with the back of his fingers. "Come on."

"Hi, you two," she said, smiling. Her voice overflowed with exuberance and delight. "You don't have to go."

"Oh, yes, we do."

She smiled back, impossible to hide her happiness at seeing Jack again. "Are you all right?" she asked, looking at each of them in turn, ending up with Jack, studying him.

"We'll see you later, Linda," Doc said. "We're glad to be back. You're a sight to behold, as usual."

"Better stick around," she said, struggling between joy and warning, trying not to smile so her words meant what they said.

Doc glanced at Jack. "We'll be back."

"No, really," she insisted. Then she turned to Jack. "You haven't been to your cabin, have you?"

"No, we came straight here. Why?"

She glanced down the road toward town. "Come on inside."

"What's the matter, Linda?" Jack repeated, searching her face for a clue.

Her eyes moved against her will to the center of town

again. "Nothing that can't wait until we're inside," she said, taking Jack's arm. She turned to Doc and Davy. "You too."

Jack glanced at Doc and back to Linda. "If there's something wrong, let's hear it."

"Jack," she said, her blue eyes soft and true on him, "you've had a long ride. It's hot out here. I just want you to rest a little. I'm glad you're back, really glad. I've been worried about all of you. We haven't heard anything for weeks. It must be months by now, since you left. I want to hear it from all of you. So come on in. I'll make you something cool to drink, something to eat too." She stood there with a smile on her face, but the welcome had been replaced by persuasion, and she wanted to persuade them so much that it wasn't convincing.

"We'll go in," Jack said, " but first tell us what the problem is with the cabin."

"Some things have happened recently," she said, as if she couldn't force herself to explain and she needed to detour. "Oh, come on inside, will you?" She looked to Doc for help.

"Has somebody been living in my cabin?" Jack asked, drawing her attention back to him. "Is that it? Somebody I don't know?"

"No," she said, and stepped back a few paces toward the house.

Doc dismounted, and Davy followed. "There's one way of finding out, Jack," he said, and hitched the reins to the railing. He patted his gray on the neck and stepped toward Linda.

"What's the matter?" she asked him. "You're limping."

"A little miscalculation. It's all right. Nothing serious."

"He got shot," Davy said, tying up his reins.

"Doc, are you all right?"

"We'll tell you about it inside."

Linda didn't understand. Then she studied Jack. "You're not hurt, are you?"

"I'm fine. It was Korpec," he said. "In Willow Springs. One

of them got away." It was a way of telling her that they had taken care of the situation, as well as implying that if he could come right out with it why couldn't she.

Her eyes cast a faraway look as she let her imagination linger on the threat to the lives of the men who stood before her. She stared at Jack, who mattered to her most, and walked more up the boardwalk. Then, at the base of her porch steps, she stopped and turned around, as if she had to match Jack's trust giving her his news first. In turn, she had to give hers right away. "Someone burned down your cabin."

Inside, Linda let the silence of the three men rule the house awhile. It was no time to offer them drinks and food. That impulse was long gone for them and her. Jack leaned against a side wall, Doc and Davy next to the front door. They'd been riding too long to sit down.

"I'm sorry," she said. "I didn't want to tell you, but I had to. It's terrible news for you to come home to."

"When did it happen?"

"Two days ago."

Two days seemed so close, as if the fire could have been prevented if only they had changed their schedule.

"How did it happen?" Jack asked, his eyes steady on her, his voice even. "Who did it?"

"I don't know. Nobody knows for sure. That is, nobody knows if it just burned down accidentally or what."

"One of Korpec's men got away from us," Davy told her. "Maybe he had more in him than we thought."

Jack shook his head. "I don't think it was him. He ran scared. Besides, with Korpec out of the way, he's on his own and has no real reason."

"I think Jack's right," Doc said. "That one probably is still kicking his horse to kingdom come."

"Then who's going to burn down your cabin?" Davy asked. "Who's going to do that?"

"Somebody who knew he was away," Doc said.

"That could be anybody."

"Not really."

"Besides, what for? I mean, why burn it down?"

"For any number of reasons, Davy boy. Some people don't need big reasons. Besides, *who* did it is the question."

A look of ambivalence crept into Linda's face, and although she kept following the discussion back and forth, her mind clearly was elsewhere. Jack noticed the watchfulness in her eyes as she glanced from Doc to Davy. "What is it, Linda?"

"Oh, nothing," she said. "It's something else. Nothing related to this. I really hate to give you all this at the same time. It's Sam," she said, glancing at Davy.

"What about him?" Davy asked, perking up from a slump.

"Oh, he's all right," she said, realizing that how she said it was misleading.

"What about him?" Davy asked again.

"He's in town, with his friends. He's been making a lot of noise lately about everything. He's making his presence known, to say the least."

The room fell silent, and the silence spoke of the whirl of unfriendly thoughts.

"What's he doing here?" Davy asked.

"I don't know."

"How long has he been here?" Jack said.

Linda shrugged to make the answer causal, but it was futile. "A couple of days. I know what you're thinking," she said, catching Jack's eye first and then the other two men's as they stood across from her in the front room.

"Sam did it, didn't he?" Davy said, jumping to the conclusion.

"I didn't say that, and nobody knows for sure about anything like that."

"He did it."

"Nobody knows," Linda repeated. "They're just two unrelated events that happened, that's all."

"No, it isn't. He did it. My stupid goddamn brother burned down Jack's cabin." He turned and faced the wall, avoiding Jack's eyes.

"If he did it," Doc asked, "why would he stay around?" But the tone of his question betrayed his real thoughts about it.

"Because he's stupid, that's why," Davy snapped, turning back around. He spread his hands for some sense to come of this. "Why would he do that? What's the matter with him?"

Jack now understood Linda's work to get the three of them inside her house where they would be in the homey surroundings of civilized life, the emblems of home life that should hold them back from rushing pell-mell and outraged into the street and saloon. He remembered too how she kept looking down the road when they first talked. Now he knew the reason. But she hadn't realized all that happened to them while they were gone, especially to Davy. They hadn't told her yet of their meeting with Sam, that he was wanted for murder, and that he was running loose.

"I know he did it," Davy said, the heat rising in his face. "That's what he would do—burn down his uncle's cabin. My brother. My own brother."

"Is he still in town?" Jack asked.

"He's been making a lot of noise," she said, the restraint and diversion again showing how much she knew Jack, how much she tried not to trespass against the privacy and independence of his life. "He's just a young man with lots of energy."

"He's been raising hell, hasn't he?" Jack asked, his voice even and restrained, holding back the anger.

"Well . . ." The oblique way she said it meant that, yes, he was giving people in town a hard time.

"He's at the Road's End, isn't he?"

Linda wasn't going to lie to him, he knew that. She was just going to slow them all down as much as she could. She didn't want anybody hurt. She wanted the guns to stay in their holsters.

Davy yanked open the door. His face was aflame with the outrage of betrayal. His other hand made sure that his gun was there. "I'm going to get him."

CHAPTER 20

JACK was right behind him. "Wait!" Davy hesitated long enough to reveal the uncertainty of his loyalties. He stood motionless in the doorway, his back rigid, head faced away to the self-respect that beckoned him. The silence behind him meant that all eyes were on his next move.

He turned around and showed the mix of intense anger and humiliation over his blood association with Sam. The combination was dangerous, because it was fused by inexperience and pride. The anguish in his eyes dampened Jack's anger, as if the younger version of Jack Tyson were standing in front of him. Davy was forced to face the three of them and know that his own brother was causing havoc on the man who taught him to be himself, a man who also was a blood link to Sam and him. He had to be a man himself. He had to make up to his uncle for what his brother had inflicted.

"Where're you going?" Jack asked.

"To get Sam. That's what I said."

"It's my cabin."

"It's my brother."

They said nothing more until Doc stepped toward Davy and opened the door wider. "Come on back in."

Davy stood firm. "He's my brother, and I have to take care of this myself."

"How are you going to take care of it?" Jack asked.

"That's my problem."

"It's our problem."

Linda stepped next to Doc. "Come back in, Davy," she coaxed, concern on her face. "Please? Just for a while."

For a while made sense to him, but the longer the three of

them waited, the shorter grew his staying power. He looked from one to the other. Then pride refired the stubbornness in him, and he bolted once more against the pressure of good sense. "I have to do this."

"You don't have to prove anything," Jack said.

"You'd do it."

"Not half-cocked like this."

"I'm taking him back. I swear. I'm going to straighten him out before the law catches up to him and he ends up behind bars, or gets hanged. What about Rab Wood? He'll track him down sooner or later, convict him, and hang him. Won't he?" Davy turned on his heel, his boots sounding hard on the porch and down the steps.

"Jack," Linda said, her eyes pleading, "You've got to stop him."

Jack rushed to the door. "Davy," he called, his voice strong and harsh. "Wait right there."

Doc and Linda followed him out the door and down the steps to the horses. They gathered around the kid, corralling him before he had a chance to mount. He hung on to the reins as if the others were going to pull them out of his hands.

"You're not going alone," Jack said, no two ways about it. "Ease off."

"I'm going, Jack, and I'm going to take my goddamn brother home," he said. At the center of the storm, he had a telltale awareness that he was swearing in front of a woman, Jack's woman, and this wasn't right for him.

The crack was for the wedge of prudence that Jack used. "All right, fair enough," he said, nodding. "That's what you should do. And you're probably right. I'd do the same thing."

Linda stood next to Jack and nodded to Davy, reassuring him that Jack was on his side, and right. Doc, too, had the look of calm and confidence, the unhurried analysis of what best action to take.

Davy paused, awakened to a new show of support. But he waited to see what Jack was driving at. "Well, that's what I'm doing," he said, useless and limp, and moved to mount up.

"Remember, Sam has his two friends with him," Jack said. "You can do what you have to do, but we're going along to even it out. Right?"

Linda nodded that Jack was right. It was a fair bargain.

"That makes sense to me," Doc said, his objectivity reinforcing the sensible compromise. "It does."

"All right," Davy agreed, "but it's my business. It's between Sam and me and nobody else."

Jack nodded.

Davy looked to Doc for the same agreement.

Linda edged forward. "Just talk to him, Davy. That's all you can do. Don't get into trouble. I don't want any of you hurt. It's not worth it."

Halfway into town, Davy said, "Sam's turning into a thieving, cheap outlaw, and he's going to get shot if I don't get him out of here. The son-of-a-bitch brother." He kept his head straight forward, talking to himself.

Two men on the road recognized Jack and Doc and were about to greet them, but the tight-knit, intense group warned them off. The townspeople let the three of them ride past. This was no time for friendliness. The kid in the middle had too much fire in his eyes.

They dismounted in front of the Road's End and walked up the steps. At the top Davy said, as if bolstering his resolve to the last second, "I know Sam. He's had his day. He's in trouble and he's not going to get himself out of it."

They stepped to the doors, and there Davy stopped, stared over the batwings to inside the saloon, inhaled, and pushed open the doors. In expectation of facing his brother, Davy stiffened his back and squared his shoulders. His legs took on a deliberate, sure stride as he led the way into the bar.

Jack and Doc, on either side, caught the doors as Davy passed by them.

Only Hank was there. He'd been lifting a box to the side of the bar, and when he turned around and saw who came in, he smiled and raised his hand. "Jack! Doc!" he said. "You're back. Come on in. It's good to see you."

The three of them examined the four corners of the saloon, the door to the back, the benches, tables, and chairs. Nothing. Nobody.

"Come on," Hank repeated, standing there, his smile still broad and beaming. He looked over his own saloon as they did and asked, "What's the matter?"

"Where's Sam Bates?" Davy asked.

Hank looked back and forth at the three men. His smile faded at the intense lineup. "He's not here. He left. Really, he's gone. I saw him ride away."

They said nothing.

"Really."

Davy turned to Jack in frustration.

"Hello, Hank," Jack said.

The smile returned to the big-barreled bartender. "Come on," he said, "I haven't seen you in a coon's age. Sit down and cool off under the collar."

"Hank," Doc said. "How're you doing?"

"Good, real good," the bartender said, because that was what he always said.

Jack and Doc stepped to the bar, leaving Davy behind in unresolved frustration. At last the kid followed them to the bar and stood to the side of them.

"Where you been?"

"To hell and back," Doc said.

"When did Sam leave?" Davy asked, unsmiling.

"About an hour ago."

"I'm his brother."

"I know. I heard."

"Where's he headed?"

"Not far enough," Hank said.

"What do you mean?"

"Say, I have no quarrel with you. It's Davy, right? Brother or no brother, Sam and his friends push the limits, that's all. And it's not just with me."

"You don't know where he's headed?"

"He didn't leave town for good, if that's what you mean. He'll be back. He's been coming in about two or three o'clock. To get out of the sun."

"We'll wait."

Hank glanced at Jack. The tone in Davy's voice held more than normal sibling rivalry. "Well, then, what can I get you?"

"How about the rest of that bottle," Doc said, and pointed at the shelves behind the bar. "And three glasses to go with it."

Hank set the bottle and glasses on the bar. He looked at Jack and, with obvious caution, asked, "How long you been here?"

"We just rode in."

"You been at your cabin?"

"I heard."

Hank glanced at Davy, the same way that Linda had glanced against her will to the center of town when they first arrived. "I'm real sorry about that. Real sorry. There was nothing we could do about it. We had a fire brigade, but it was pretty near gone by the time we put it out. What could we do?"

"Nothing," Jack said. He grabbed the bottle and a glass and walked to the table at the far side wall. Doc and Davy took their glasses and followed. They sat down in a semicircle facing the door.

Davy reached for the bottle, but Jack hung on to it, keeping it in place at the center of the table. He shook his head. "Not now."

The glasses remained empty as they waited through the long minutes and hours.

"You sure he didn't leave town?" Davy called over to Hank.

"Not positive. He could've gone off and said nothing about it. But it sure as hell didn't look like it."

"He comes in about this time?"

"He's only been in town a couple days, you know, but he comes in two or three times a day, stirring up the dust, if there was somebody else in here to stir it up with. You're a nice kid, Davy, I don't mind saying that. But your brother is a son of a bitch. I don't mind saying that either. The two of you are night and day, as far as I'm concerned."

The three of them watched Hank wipe the top of the bar as if he were debating whether to continue with what he was saying.

Finally, he said it. "Now, I keep to my own business. *This* is my business, and I don't go around yakking about what people do. That's *their* business. You know that, Jack."

Jack nodded.

"You're a man of the cloth," Doc said, agreeing and grinning.

Hank turned a puzzled eye on him and smiled as he looked down at what he was doing. "Well, anyway, a man does what he does, just so long as everybody has a good time. But since Sam rode in here he's been causing trouble. I don't mind saying it."

"Like what?" Jack asked.

Hank stared at him. "I don't want to say," he said, the implication intended with the pause, "because I don't know for sure. But I know some other things. He went over to Mildred's, him and his men, just roaming around and pulling bolts of cloth down on the floor. So he said, 'Let's go,' and he walked with his dirty boots all over the cloth on purpose, laughing as he walked out the door. Mildred told me. And he got in a fight with Jerry. Bloodied him over nothing, just for the hell of it, I guess. Even pulled a gun on him, scaring him and his friends silly. Comes in here and plays cards so he's sure to win, if you know what I mean.

That almost started a ruckus. People here don't want no trouble, so they backed off. He was going to pull a gun. I saw it." He looked at the three men watching and listening to him. "That's what I'm talking about."

They waited another half hour, past the time Hank figured Sam would be back.

When they heard horses stopping in front of the Road's End, Davy stared at the door and listened as men dismounted, laughed, hitched the reins, and walked up the steps.

CHAPTER 21

JACK moved his chair away from the table, and Doc folded the ends of his jacket behind his holster. Davy leaned on his forearms and studied the door.

"That'll be them," Hank said from behind the bar.

The laughter and shuffle of boot steps on the boardwalk made the motionless swing doors seem all the more still. Then Sam and his two friends burst through the entrance, shoving the doors on their hinges as the three men suddenly appeared, colliding with each other, laughing and slugging each other's shoulders.

They were six feet into the saloon before they realized someone else was there. The room turned totally silent. No one moved. They were caught off guard by the way Davy, Jack, and Doc sat analyzing them, as if they'd bumbled into a trap.

Sam saw Davy first. His eyes moved to Jack, and when that happened fear drained the color from his face. He was a statue of himself, caught and undraped, surprised more than merely being thrown off guard by their presence. He was caught by the reflection of what he was in Jack's and Davy's eyes.

"Howdy, boys," Hank said, but his normal brightness wavered a bit.

Sam ignored Hank and recovered fast. He stepped to the bar and said over his shoulder, eyes still on Davy, "What're you doing here?" His friends followed him.

"Hello, Sam," Jack said, his voice flat and distant, his eyes on the three men moving across the room. The message was clear.

"Jack," Sam acknowledged.

"What are *you* doing here?" Davy asked.

"I'm getting myself a drink. I wanted to see where Jack lives. What's the matter with that?"

"You saw it, didn't you?"

"Yeah, but I heard it burned down." He turned to Jack and said, "Too bad that happened."

Jack nodded. "It's very bad it happened."

"Who did it?" Davy asked.

"How should I know? We just came through, that's all, to see what this place looked like. Now we saw it, and we're going to head out."

"Who burned Jack's cabin down?" Davy persisted.

"Don't ask me. How the hell should I know something like that? Could be anybody. I don't know. What the hell you driving at, anyway?"

"I know who burned it down," Davy said, his forearms still resting on the table in plain sight, his face cold and fixed.

Hank slipped between the pause. "What would you like, boys? Whiskey? What do you say?"

"Yeah, sure," Sam said, half turning back on Davy, half keeping himself aware of what the situation was turning into.

Hank set up a bottle and glasses and poured the whiskey for them. "Here you go," he said, sliding the glasses toward the men. "It's damn hot out there today."

"I heard what you're doing in town," Davy said with the same edge in his voice, as if Hank hadn't done or said anything.

"Heard what?" Sam asked, his confidence returning.

"It doesn't take long to stir up trouble, does it?"

"What the hell are you talking about?" Sam asked, and laughed, shaking his head.

"You know what I'm talking about. You got in a fight with someone in town, didn't you? You pulled a gun on him. What was it? Three against one?"

"I didn't pull any gun on anybody," Sam said, and took a drink. He turned to his friends and asked, "Did I do that?"

They shook their heads.

"I didn't do any damn thing like that," Sam said, forcing a smile. "You're just trying to start something. You want me to get out of here, is that it? That's what these people really want. That's why they're telling you these lies. Well, we'll go when we goddamn want to."

"You're still cheating at cards, aren't you?"

"What's the matter with you? The hell I am."

"I almost got killed because of you. You left a bad reputation behind you, and I crossed it. You cheated somebody in Big Butte, and he took it out on me."

"I can't help that. Every time somebody loses, they think I'm cheating. I just win. That makes me cheating? Hell, no, it doesn't. It makes me good at cards."

"You owe Jack a double eagle."

Sam glanced at Jack, sitting there with direct eyes on him. "What for?"

"For paying off your gambling debt."

"What debt?"

"I told you. In Big Butte."

"Then whoever it was took you for a sucker, because I won fair and square. He's lying through his teeth."

"He says you stole the money when you lost."

"The hell I did. What kind of brother are you. You take the word of some goddamn stranger over mine? Huh? Is that it?"

"You pulled a gun on him."

"I didn't pull any gun on anybody."

Davy said nothing.

Sam sniffed disgust and took another drink. "You're supposed to be my brother. Yeah."

"You're a troublemaker, Sam, and now you're wanted. There's a U.S. marshal tracking you down. If he catches up to you, he's going to hang you."

"Nobody's going to catch me for nothing."

"It's time to go back home."

"Go to hell."

"It's time to go back," Davy repeated. He shoved his chair back, stood up, and took a step toward Sam.

At once Sam set his glass down on the bar and set his legs ready. His two friends stood out from the bar.

Jack put his right hand on his thigh close to his holster. Doc moved his feet into position for standing up.

The two pairs of men bristled at each other in the silence that separated them.

"All right, boys, all right," Hank said, raising his hand for peace. "Now, come on. No trouble in here. You hear me? I don't want any trouble in my place. This is a good place. Now just take it easy, all of you. All of you, just take it easy."

"It's between Sam and me," Davy said to Hank, keeping his eyes on his brother.

"Then keep it that way," Hank said.

Davy put his hand to his side, motioning at Jack and Doc. "Keep out of it," he told them, again keeping his eyes on Sam. He waited and lifted his head to get the same pledge from Sam's friends.

Jack and Doc stood up in slow motion and moved back to the wall, separating themselves as they went.

"Yeah," Sam said to his men, "stay out of it."

His friends stepped out of the way, both of them watching Jack and Doc across the room like partners in a mean square dance.

Davy took two steps in a circle to the left of Sam and stopped. "You're coming back with me before you get hanged."

"Who says? I cut loose when I left the farm, and I'm my own out here. I'm a free man here, and nobody is going to come out and tell me what to do."

"Mother is worried about you."

"To hell with her."

Davy's eyes flared white heat. "What'd you say?" he shouted, and stepped closer.

"You heard me. To hell with her."

"Goddamn you, Sam. They're going to *hang* you. You're a killer. You don't care about anybody but yourself and what you can get and steal. Only, you're stealing from all of us."

"Shut your goddamn mouth."

Hank pressed against the shelf of bottles. Jack and Doc kept watch on Sam's cronies. Nobody moved fast, nobody moved slow.

"You don't belong here," Davy said, and stepped closer. "You're pulling your gun on people. You killed a man. You're turning no good."

"You goddamn hypocrite," Sam shouted, pointing at Davy's gun. "You're so goddamn innocent. *You're* carrying a gun. How many men you killed? Huh?"

Davy stared at him. "I'm taking you back."

"Go ahead," Sam said, seeing the taunt making a mark, "tell me why you're carrying a gun. Because you'd kill your own brother, wouldn't you? You'd kill your own brother, or you wouldn't be carrying it. Goddamn right. You going to shoot me?"

"I'm going to beat the hell out of you."

When Davy lunged for Sam, his friends stepped forward, hands by their sides.

Jack and Doc did the same.

Hank yelled, "Hey!" and the men stayed in place.

Davy shoved his open palm into Sam's shoulder, sending his brother sprawling. Sam sprung back and swung his fist at Davy's head, grazing it above the ear and sending Davy to the side.

Anger seized Davy full force. He charged with his whole weight at Sam, crashing his shoulder into Sam's gut and wrapping his arms around Sam's legs, squeezing the air from his brother's lungs, lifting him off the floor and smashing him with all his weight onto the floor. The only trouble was that Davy went with him.

Sam rolled over and flailed at Davy's head, hitting once, missing twice.

Davy connectd with a fist at Sam's forehead, sending Sam reeling back hard enough for Davy to follow with another blow to the head, sending him against the floor again.

Davy crawled on top of Sam's chest, pressed his forearm into Sam's neck, and with the other hand slapped Sam's face back and forth hard, twice, three times, the sound of the blows loud, painful, and humiliating.

Sam kicked one knee into Davy's back. It did no good. He kicked again more wildly, and this time Davy's back arched with the pain. He let loose of his forearm pressed against Sam's throat. Sam twisted fast and slugged his brother in the solar plexus, crushing the air out of Davy. Then he beat his fists twice on the side of Davy's head, breaking the skin. Blood splattered on the floor.

Davy twisted free, fueled by outrage. He shoved Sam to the floor. Then he got to his feet, reached down, grabbed Sam by the collar, and yanked him to his feet. With one hand, he choked the shirt around Sam's throat. With the other, he cocked his fist to his ear and sprung loose, smashing his knuckles into Sam's cheek so hard that he lost his grip on the shirt.

Sam came back with a wild glancing blow at Davy's shoulder.

The other men stood on a knife edge of danger, guarding the two bleeding brothers flailing at each other, their fists against bone and flesh filling the room with the punishing sound.

Sam's fist punched Davy's head, only this time was different. This time the force caught Davy off balance. His legs couldn't hold the sudden thrust of the rest of his body. He teetered and fell backward, his arms and hands clutching nothing but air, his legs useless against the propulsion of his torso. His head hit the edge of the bar with the full weight of his collapsing body. The hardwood edge hit his neck at the base of his skull, and the sound terrified everyone.

CHAPTER 22

THE hush that filled the room centered on Davy, crumpled at the foot of the bar. The men stared at the kid, and the time it took for anyone to move stretched to eternity.

Sam stared at his brother, fear and disbelief in his face. His fists still were clenched from the killing blow, his legs still bent with the strength of attack.

With the same fear and disbelief on his face, he turned to Jack and searched for a clue to what had happened. The terror in his eyes overflowed with the dread of all that Jack saw in him and what Jack would do to him. "It was an accident," Sam said, helpless fear his only recourse, his only justification.

Jack's hand hung by his holster, his eyes murderous.

But he didn't draw.

The room waited on Jack's move, as if he alone had the final right—the only right.

The men stood their ground against each other, waiting for Jack in these hot seconds.

Then one of Sam's cronies sensed the danger of remaining there a minute longer. "Sam," he said in a low, sharp, awakening warning. He got Sam's eye and jerked his head to go, leave fast, get out of there while they could.

It was up to Sam. He moved in slow motion, almost in remorse and abjectness—but the fear was there. He had done something horrible and irreversible, and the fortune of his own life depended on running away. He released his clenched fists and backed off with caution, as if Jack was the tiger of outraged anger ready to claw him to death if he made a single wrong move, a single smart-mouth miscalculation.

His friends backed off the same way, both of them stepping with the same slow, deliberate moves.

Doc wore the ready gunning look in his eye and hand, but it was Jack's move that would signal Doc to draw the judgment on Sam.

The fight was inside Jack. The war was between the fury of revenge and the death of another one of the bloodline. Davy was the innocence of his own life. Sam wasn't, but he was Davy's brother. The horrendous injustice of Davy's chance death would have been an easy matter to settle if Sam weren't of the same family line. One side of Jack impelled him to batter Sam to death as Sam had Davy. The other side held off because he would be battering his own life.

Sam backed to the door. His face of fear and terror still showed what he had done. How much of it was fear of Jack, how much the horror at the death of his own brother by his own hand, was impossible to tell. "It was an accident," he pleaded. And disappeared.

They buried Davy in the Caliente cemetery, a stark and lonely hilltop of wooden crosses with rough-hewn names and dates. A few townspeople came because they were friends of Jack. He and Doc shoveled dirt onto the grave and the pine box, the pebbles pinging on the wood at first, and then the people left.

The sun beat down on them. The hilltop was dry and dusty, the air oppressive. The heat of the day had accumulated and was shimmering on the distant land.

Together Jack and Doc patted down the mound of the grave with the backs of their shovels. Then they stood with Linda, the three of them looking at the grave, tears in her eyes for Jack, the one she loved.

To Jack, the land around him was a vast maker of men. Everywhere he looked the earth seemed fertile ground for new lives, and what a man brought to it was what he could make of himself. If he brought emptiness, he'd end up empty. If he brought the seed of a town, he'd end up making a town like Caliente, or any number of settlements in the culverts of the West, from shack towns to Dodge Cities.

Davy came to Jack and the West not just to find his brother Sam. He came hoping to become a man, and he looked to Jack for paternal lessons.

Jack had no idea how he could tell his sister Jessica. She would be devastated by the news. That Davy was killed by his own brother would be an incalculable agony for Jessica. She wouldn't believe the accident of it, only the Cain and Abel of it, son against son.

Jack stepped away from the grave. The land he looked at was not only a maker of men, it was a burier of men. A nameless, infinite grave. He hated the country for what it did to Davy. The West had changed Jack to the roots; here, he had learned to survive, but he'd failed to teach Davy the same lesson.

The openness of the country let men like him and Davy grow fast and free. Maybe that was the flaw. Maybe that was the warning—you had to be disciplined and tempered, like metal, controlling your potential in order to make it last.

He didn't hate this country, he knew that. He hated what it could inflict, by design and by chance. That was the risk of the land to the men who fed off it, and that was the magnetism holding him to it.

"Jack?" Linda asked, her voice tentative and careful.

He heard her over his own inner voice. Davy had the core of a solid man in him, but his innocence turned ambitious and prideful. The kid grew enamored of his natural talent of hand to gun, too absorbed in his quick successes, and too confident in them. The temptation to be more than what he was led him to cross the line to what he wasn't. Jack should have done something about that, but he was too aware of trespass, too mindful of wanting to give the kid plenty of room—another flaw of unbridled freedom that went with this country.

It wasn't too late for Jack to go after Sam. He would finish what Davy set out to accomplish with such passion. He would track down Sam no matter what and straighten him out. Maybe he'd do it from his own guilt, but he'd do it.

"Jack?" Linda called again.

This time he turned to her. "I have to go after Sam."

"I know," she said. In one look she conveyed all the understanding he needed. She knew that he had within him the power to keep his gun away from Sam, and that he was ruled by more than a trigger and a bullet.

"I'm going with you," Doc said.

Jack hesitated. He was the one who had to take care of Sam, and the impulse to do it alone appealed to his sense of justice. But that was the temptation of fools and the innocent. "Yeah, all right."

"Good," Doc said, slapping him on the shoulder. "That's the plan for tomorrow. Now, what about today? Your cabin's burned down. Where are you going to stay until we get it rebuilt?"

Linda reached her open hand to Jack, and he took it. They both knew this finally was their time.